To L.
The p.v.
Sanlarpios, thanks for being
a good sport!

[signature]

MIAMI
UNDERGROUND

MARC ZAPPULLA

MIAMI UNDERGROUND

This is a work of fiction. As in all fiction, literary insights and perceptions are based on experiences. Therefore all names, characters, places and incidents are a product of the author's imagination or are used fictitiously. Any resemblance to actual persons, living or deceased, events or locales is entirely coincidental.

Published in the United States by
True Emperor Publishing, Inc.

ISBN: 1794192201
ISBN 13: 9781794192201
Library of Congress Control Number
Kindle Direct Publishing Platform

Cover art and design © 2019 by Mike Petrillo

MARC ZAPPULLA

ACKOWLEDGEMENTS

Mom and dad, with your encouragement, love and support, I feel like I can conquer the world. Thank you for everything, I love you both very much. To my best friends and story contributors, Peter Morel and Phil Yebba for your creativity, guidance, and unrelenting support from beginning to end. A big thanks to my friend, Mike Petrillo, for his outstanding work once again in designing a book cover that's such an inspiring work of art, and one that will be celebrated for years to come. To my beloved nieces and nephews Timmy, Sarah, Isabella, and JoJo, I love you all, don't ever grow up. To the rest of my family and close friends for your continued loyalty and support. I wouldn't be here without you. So thank you. I love you all. Lastly, a special thank you to The Villa Casa Casuarina for your beauty, elegance, and historical richness; Google, Amazon, Amazon Kindle and Kindle KDP for your outstanding professionalism, insight, and logistical work in getting this book off the ground.

Gold is a treasure, and he who possesses it does all he wishes to in this world, and succeeds in helping souls into paradise.

—Christopher Columbus

CHAPTER 1

THE BOY

He is just a boy, barely eight years of age. Yet there he is in the corner of the cargo hold, tiny and frail, draped in tattered clothes, crouched in a tight fetal position with his head craned low, unwilling to correct his position and address the one who speaks to him.

"So, little one, you were the one helping yourself to the all the bananas, huh?" says Gussy Fitzpatrick, standing over the boy. Gussy is a longshoreman, a 10-year veteran of the Boston waterfront, and the last to leave the ship after several hours of unloading produce onto the pier with his gang (a group of longshoremen assigned to work together as a unit on a particular task).

"What's your name, kid?" The boy remains still and silent. "Go on, you can tell me, it's OK, you're not in any trouble."

After a few moments, Gussy jests, "If only my ex-wife were this quiet, we'd still be together." It was a joke that, not surprisingly, did not land. He then stoops to within a couple of feet from the boy, and from his bent-knees position, he softens his voice and says, "Does your daddy work on the ship?"

The boy finally engages, though shyly and quietly, by shaking his head.

"OK, we're getting somewhere," said Gussy. "Do you have a daddy?"

The boy shakes his head again.

"A mommy?"

Same response. Just then, however, as sudden as a lightning strike, the boy unknots himself and leaps into Gussy's arms and tightly wraps himself around his shoulders.

"Jesus," says Gussy as he holds the boy in his arms. "Come on, I'll take you home with me."

Gussy stands with the boy clinging to him and walks out of the cargo hold, off the ship and eventually off the pier.

It's a dilapidated tenement, to say the least. The hallways reek of sour food, foul body stench, and decomposing rodents. There is a communal toilet that lacked the basic amenities, including a working sink to wash up after one's business is completed. The tenants couldn't afford toilet paper, so in an effort to cut costs, they saved the wrappings used to cover the fruits and vegetables they bought and used them to wipe. They came in several bright colors and were stacked directly to the left of the porcelain on a splintery wooden shelf.

On Sundays, the "Bone Man" would pull up in front of the building on his horse and cart and call out, "Bones! Bones! Who's got bones?" He was looking for the leftover bones from the meat: Chicken, turkey, beef, etc. They were used to make soap. Some would toss them right out of the window and into the cart, while others came outside with a bag or other mode of carrying and dump the bones in, then going back inside.

"This is your new home...at least for now," said Gussy, all the while not knowing how a boy so young, presumably from the United Kingdom (as that's where the ship came from), ended up fighting for his survival alone in a depths of a dirty old ship. The answers will come, but not yet.

The boy, in the meantime, is emotionless. His only reaction to his new digs was his unenthusiastic gaze panning the room. He holds his sight on the bed, walks to it and sits, then makes himself comfortable by curling back into a fetal position and closing his eyes.

CHAPTER 2

JAKE

It's been nearly 30 years since Jake Kelly was rescued by his guardian, Gussy, whom he now considers his Pops.

Today Jake is a bruiser. He's 5'11, ruggedly handsome, wide-standing and packed full of British muscle.

It's springtime and the year is 2017. At Title Boxing Club on Causeway Street in Boston, Jake is dancing in the ring, snapping off jab after jab with his left while following each toss with an occasional power-punch with his right. His vision is narrow as he focuses on his opponent, his sparring partner, Big Willy Steed. Willy is a house, standing 6'2 with broad shoulders, tree-stump legs and enormous arms. He's wrapped by an extra layer of fat pushing him over the 250-pound mark, and it's enough for him to tire in the third round against a much lighter, quicker, and more ferocious Jake.

Kelly, once nicknamed The British Assassin, was a contender in the light middleweight division of the British Army until a scrappy southpaw from East London saw an opening in his defenses and delivered a life-altering blow to the head that knocked him to the canvas and sidelined him for good. That was 18 years ago. Today, however, at the age of 38, he's in rhythm, in a zone while getting a few rounds in against his hefty opponent.

Once honorably discharged from the United Kingdom Special Forces, he settled back in, in the States in Boston alongside Gussy as a longshoreman, where he learned how to operate a crane and forklift, and develop a web of intricate strategies that earned him the title "Best Whist Player on the Docks."

Although his physical toughness and superb card playing skills are well documented in the ring and on the waterfront, what he's truly known for is his ability to steal. And he learned from the best—from Gussy. His Pops taught him the basics on how to lift cargo from the ships, directly from the pier or from the storage warehouse, and how to hide his tracks, so not even the most keenly suspicious person could uncover any evidence. Gussy, in fact, once watched his own friend, a man named Tony Costa, pull off the heist of the century back in the mid-seventies. It was a barrel of gold shavings taken right out of the warehouse. Gussy would often remind Jake that "Tony Costa was a man to admire."

So Jake took all he knew, his teachings from Gussy, his experiences in the military, and his nerve, and now commands an uber-talented team of thieves that includes three others, all of whom have their own role in the gang and dutifully assist in sizable thefts of diamonds, gold, art, or any nature of high-priced collectibles with price tags ranging from several hundred thousand to several millions.

And while his day job does afford an abundance of opportunities to steal all kinds of cargo coming and going from the port of Boston, his crew never takes anything right from the docks. Jake's rule, in place and unbroken since the gang took their first piece of metal just over ten years ago. The reason: He never wanted to bring unwanted heat on the pier as a result of his "side business." He didn't think it seemed fair to the rest of the longshoremen who also wanted their share of the cargo coming and going.

Conversely, Jake the individual lifted scores of items off the waterfront, and was aided many times by Gussy. In the streets, though, as a young man, given his and Gussy's circumstances, continuously flirting with the poverty line, Jake stole anything he could get his hands on, from a bag of peanuts out of a five-and-dime store to cars parked against the curb in plain view (when he was twelve and could finally reach the pedals). And it was all done in the name of survival.

In the ring it's round four, and Jake is quick to go to work on Willy until his peripheral vision catches a bald, stumpy figure in an overcoat and fedora approaching from his right. The man's right hand is holding a small, folded piece of paper between his thumb and index finger. Jake extends his left arm to Willy to indicate the stop sign. A gassed Willy happily retreats back to his corner, while Jake makes his way to the ropes where the portly fellow offers the note.

"What took you so long?" a hard-breathing Jake inquires in his well-maintained British accent. Jake takes the message.

"Hey," said Paulie, "I can only move as fast as the guys above me."

"And do me a favor, stop comin' around here dressed like Vito Corleone, for Christ's sake." Jake went on. "You see anyone around here lookin' like you, mate?"

"Hey, I don't see anyone opening up their mouth about it, but you, and you should mind your own business."

Jake unfolds the note, snickers to suggest a nonsensical message is before him. He hands it back to

Paulie. "Burn it, these notes are pointless and stupid. Just tell me what you want."

"How about I wipe my ass with it?"

"If you can reach it, by all means." Jake said.

"Fuck you!" Paulie countered. "And by the way, I'll be back in a couple of weeks with another note."

"Don't bother, we're done," said Jake, "We're taking a break."

"Don't tell me, tell Nick, he runs the show."

"I did," he said, "but aren't you the messenger boy, anyway?"

"You know, you really are a punk, "said Paulie. "Is everyone an asshole where you're from?" He turns to Willy, who's still catching his breath, and says, "Knock this bum out, will ya?" Willy sluggishly raises his right arm as if to say he'll do his best.

"Willy," said Jake, "Let's go!"

A visibly disgusted Willy props himself up slowly using the ropes as leverage, then meets Jake in the middle of the ring in a fatigue-laden pose, nods, and proceeds to take his beating.

CHAPTER 3

CHOPS

Over in Cambridge, Massachusetts, Professor Douglas McMasters is teaching philosophy at Harvard University. Despite his scholarly demeanor and preppy outer appearance, Douglas is not just any Ivy League educator; in fact, his real name isn't even Douglas, or McMasters, it's Jeffrey "Chops" Turner. Chops is a nickname he picked up as a kid thanks to his intense obsession with Bruce Lee and the power of his karate chop. It spurred him to take karate lessons for several years, though he never could get past the yellow belt. Nonetheless, Chops is Jake's most trusted member of his gang of thieves. He's invaluable because of his unmatched ability to cloak his identity and run such superb reconnaissance missions, all by use of his clandestine, unassuming and non-threatening demeanor…and his Nikon camera.

He'd met Jake when they were in adjacent cells at the county lockup in Boston. Jake was in for a simple assault; Chops for forging his mom's boyfriend's signature on a credit card receipt at a sex toy shop. It was a deliberate attempt to get the guy in trouble and hope his mom would send him packing, as Chops wasn't a big fan of him, or anyone his mother dated for that matter. Unfortunately, his plan backfired—not because the signature wasn't sound, but because he eventually learned that his mom and the boyfriend were both regular patrons of the store. Even so, he spent thirty days inside when his own mother pressed charges. When he came out, he and Jake began chumming around. But it wasn't until Chops got the job at Harvard that Jake realized how special he was.

It began with an identity adjustment, because his own, no thanks to his wayward history, was not going to cut it. So he changed his name, created fake transcripts, job history, references; he even videotaped himself giving a brilliant lecture on philosophy and complexity in reasoning. And all of this was all just a precaution, a just-in-case in the event someone at the school wanted to be a hero and go down the rabbit-hole of fact-checking his existence.

His mission: to first follow the Chair of the Arts and Sciences Department, Tom Ford. And he did, a lot; to and from work, to his favorite bar, favorite restaurant he and his wife frequented, and he kept watching, taking pictures and documenting everything. He was the perfect mark because he heard the rumors about a "perv" faculty member when he bugged an oft-reserved table for the city's high society members at a bar on Beacon Hill. One patron, a city council member, spilled his guts about Ford and his penchant for cozying up with female students off-campus. Thus, Ford became the "low-hanging fruit" to extort.

The operation had borne little fruit, until he saw Ford head for a motel with a little blonde coed in tow. *Too easy*, he thought. However, it did take a few months, but Chops got him by taking several compromising pictures of the two coming and going from the motel, as well as having sex in his car. The evidence was strong and undeniable, and would give even to the most staunch defense attorney a fit. But it wasn't enough, not for Chops. So he went after the president of the university, Charles Tananbaum.

Tananbaum was a horse of a different color. He was a pillar of the educational community. He'd received several honorary awards for excellence, and had even been invited to speak at the Democratic National Convention in 1992. Among all of his brightest accolades lies a dark cloud: he has a very, very bad gambling habit that landed him in some boiling-hot water with a bookie working out of Providence, RI.

Tananbaum was short some change and put it off a little too long for the bookie's taste, and so they caught up with him as he was putting his keys in the driver's side door of his 7-Series BMW in the parking lot of the Rockingham Race Track in Salem, NH. It just so happened Chops had a bird's-eye view and caught the whole thing on his camera. The men gave him a stern talking-to along with a few open-handed slaps to the face he'd find difficult to explain to others. When the gangsters got back in their big black Lincoln Town Car, Chops sprang out of his late model, blue Honda Accord and over to Tananbaum and said, "Sir, I just want you to know I saw everything, and if you need me to be a witness, I will gladly testify on your behalf, in fact…"

Charles' face was beet-red, puffy and bruised, he was breathing heavily and grew increasingly anxious by the second and responded, "No, no. I really appreciate that, young man, but there's no need. They won't be back."

"Are you sure?" said Chops. "Because I have their license plate and physical descriptions, along with the photos I took of you speaking with them." He went on, "I have some audio as well, not from today, but it's good. There's some static, but I'm sure when the cops examine it they'll be able to transcribe it with little difficulty."

"Who in God's name are you, son?" asked Charles in great disbelief.

"I'm your new professor. My name is Je... Douglas McMasters. I'll see you on Monday at about 10:00 a.m....I have a meeting with your chair at 9. I'll have my credentials with me...and yours, for that matter. And I expect a healthy salary. I know you Harvard types, you're tighter than a duck's ass in water. It's time to open up the vault."

"My schedule is full, son."

"No, it's not," said Chops. "Jennifer, your pretty little secretary does a horrible job keeping your schedule a secret...in fact, sometimes she leaves it right on your desk when you're not even there."

"You're insane."

"No, I'm just a guy with a hell of a lot of ambition," Chops went on. "Now, if I were you I'd take care of that eye before it swells up like a beach ball. You don't want the wife to worry too much. Hey, you know, we should do coffee some time, though. Maybe you, me, and that treasury guy you're always talking to about getting a loan from the school funds. Anyway, you think about it." Chops continued, "And by the way, don't mess with me, Chucky. I took karate for eight years and chopped my way through the streets of Boston as a kid."

Chops runs off, stops and turns back to him, and says, "I'm really excited we're going to be working together!"

Tananbaum's mouth was agape, but he was speechless, as he just endured perhaps the worst day of his life.

Ten years later, the still boyish-looking Chops, who's now 35 years old, is giving a lesson on leadership to a packed auditorium of students when someone knocks on the door, grabbing everyone's attention. "Anyone order pizza?" Chops suggests kiddingly, drawing a chuckle from the audience. "Come in!"

The door opens, and there is President Tananbaum walking prudently toward Chops, so as to not disappointment him.

"Everyone," said Chops, "You all know President Tananbaum."

"Hello, kids," Charles says.

"And to what do we owe the pleasure of your visit, sir?"

"I am truly, truly sorry for interrupting you, Professor, but there is a man on the phone for you named Jake," he said skittishly, with his shoulders hunched forward in an uneasy posture. "For some reason he insisted on having me fetch you in person. I hope that is acceptable?"

"Of course it is, President Tananbaum." said Chops. "Turn to page 76, please," he called out to the class. "Let's walk to your office, shall we?"

"After you, professor" said the president.

The two enter the office. Chops places himself in Tananbaum's chair, picks up the phone and punches Line 1. Tananbaum stands and looks on, quietly and uncomfortably.

"What's up, bro?" said Chops to Jake. "Sure thing," he says, and then hangs up the phone.

"That's it?" asks Tananbaum.

"That's it, my friend."

CHAPTER 4

TIM "ROBBY" CANE

He's bold and brash, charismatic and handsome as a prince. Along with Tim Cane's movie-star looks and unyielding charm, he's quick-handed and could pick the pocket of a heavily guarded luminary with a simple handshake and a hello. Hence the nickname "Robby." So, it warranted no real shock when Jake offered him a spot in his then-growing band of "takers."

Oddly enough, the two men clashed one evening when they were both attempting to lift the same pricy pendant encased at Manhattan Jewelry in downtown Boston. Robby arrived first and had disabled the alarm, thanks to his wooing of the store manager and all he learned from her after a few drinks and a night of mind-blowing sex. He walked away with her electronic keycard, which gained him entry into the place. But more importantly, the small piece of plastic turned the elegantly shiny depot into a dark abyss when placed just a few inches from a designated spot beneath the cash register. Jake, realizing he'd been outdone at that moment, cautiously entered anyway to see Robby holding the pendant high above his head and laughing sinisterly until suddenly he hears the sound of a pistol being cocked just inches from his right ear. Robby separates his hands slowly to assume a retreating stance.

Jake took the pendant from him.

"You're not security," said Robby.

"No," replied Jake.

"Then who are you?"

"You can put your hands down," commanded Jake.

Robby obliged.

"You did all of this on your own?" Jake said, gesturing with his gun.

"Yes."

Jake said, "I'm impressed.

"Thank you."

"You wanna work for me?"

"Sure."

"You're hired on one condition."

"What's that?" asked Robby.

"Hand me back my wallet or I'll blow your fuckin' brains out right here, mate."

Robby happily accommodated the request and said, "You're good."

Jake lowered the weapon and said, "We'll be in touch."

"We'll be in touch?" asked Robby.

"That's right."

Jake then walks backwards and slowly while keeping the gun on Robby. He reaches the door, turns, opens it and leaves. Robby's expression is hopeless, but soon transforms into promise.

That was five years ago. Today Robby is sitting at a diner in South Boston and finishing up his breakfast. The phone in the restaurant rings a few times before a woman waddles behind the counter and answers it. After a moment she calls out, "Is there a Robby Cane here?"

Robby shifts his sitting position toward the counter, a confused look overcoming his expression. He raises his right arm uncertainly and says, "Did you say Robby Cane?"

"Yes, are you he?"

"Yes."

"Phone's for you," the woman said. Come on up, sugar, I ain't got all day."

So he does. Robby walks away from his booth and to the counter. The woman stretches the cord and hands him the phone. He answers, "Hello?" A few seconds elapses before he says, "Sure thing," then hands it back to the woman.

He retreats back to his booth, takes a sip of his coffee, and leans back with a grin. A pretty young waitress hands him the bill with a great big smile and says, "Will that be all, darling?"

"Oh, um, yes, it is, sorry, my mind was elsewhere for a second."

"Not a problem," she said, placing the bill receipt in front of him. "Take your Time."

"Thank you," he said as he instinctively turns the bill over and sees a phone number with the name 'Tiffany' just below it, and a drawn-in heart below that.

"The day keeps getting better," Robby says to himself.

CHAPTER 5

HENRY "MAC" HUCKABEE

Only a pair of stock cars sits on the treacherous dirt track known as the Devil's Bowl Speedway. Aesthetically, the autos seem to represent a long history of brutish-style racing with many setbacks to go along with it, but the revving of the engines suggest the vehicles are ready for more. They're lined up side-by-side, each with a driver draped in a tattered racing suit, capped by a helmet and visor. Sitting in the left position is Henry Huckabee, a technology expert and gambling junkie with an affinity for thrill-seeking on the racetracks. Henry actually goes by Mac. The nickname was actually given to him by Jake, who was so ultra-impressed with his technological prowess, he decided to name him after the Mac computer.

Mac is also a Georgia Tech dropout who found it more fulfilling to use his talents for evil than for personal or professional growth. In point of fact, he once dubbed in a previously recorded phone call into the quarterback's helmet mic of his girlfriend talking dirty to his running back, thus causing him to throw the game-losing interception in the Rose Bowl.

The technical wonder honed his skills when he developed his very own hacking software, which consequently was a mixture of the top features from some of the more popular ones out there, and just as effective. The one discernible difference is Mac's signature technology. He placed a boomerang module in it so when a person or organization attempts to identify his software as a threat, it hits back and delivers a virus called Uncle Freddy's Cockeyed Bitch, appropriately named after his Uncle Freddy's ex-girlfriend, who was cockeyed and a major bitch, according to Uncle Freddy. The software itself was named Darth Henry. He used Darth Henry to deliberately crash a cruise ship into Boston Harbor after he complained about a price adjustment just before he tried to book a vacation with the cruise line. Luckily, there were no serious injuries on the ship or the docks, but it was a felony, and Mac paid the price. When he was released, Jake sought him out and offered him a job. He gleefully accepted.

He never did book that cruise.

On the track and to the right of Mac is another driver, #5; an unwitting test subject who's in the race to win a bet between him and Mac: a winner-take-all of $5,000.

He gives the thumbs-up to his crew full of rejects, four strong. In front of them is a young, beautiful blonde girl in pigtails sporting Daisy Dukes and holding a Confederate flag handkerchief high above her head with her left hand. She shouts, "Ready! Set! Go!"

The cars spin their wheels, tossing a hail mud before steadying their traction and taking off. The blonde shrieks in excitement as the cars rumble past her, spraying mud all over her golden locks as she laughs hysterically while simultaneously shields herself from the debris as it covers her.

The cars bang and crunch at every turn. The track is fierce and rigid, and bent with lots of corners and small hills, or jumps if one finds enough momentum.

Mac is finding enjoyment, hooting with every turn of the wheel, while his opponent is stone-faced, chasing the $5,000 purse like a hound in pursuit of a hare. Then suddenly, Mac raises a small detonator with a push-button at its top. "So long, asshole!" he shouts at the other driver. He presses the button with his thumb, subsequently shutting down every working function in car #5, stopping it in its tracks.

"What the fuck?!" #5 shouts. "Damn it!" He slams the wheel with both hands.

As Mac turns back, cackling, marveling at his achievement, his attention takes him too far away from the road, and so he steers straight when the track calls for a right turn and subsequently crashes into a wall, provoking the car to overturn and flip several times until its erraticism is stopped by an incline off the road. It skids softly to a halt. Mac remains seated and securely strapped in, but upside down and wincing in pain.

"Boss!" a member of his crew calls out. "Boss! Are you OK?" The bellows become louder and closer until Reggie, a young black teenaged kid, is kneeling and tilting his head to communicate with his driver. "Are you OK, boss?" he asked one more time, near breathless.

"Did I win?"

"Technically, no. No one did."

"Fuck me," says Mac.

"But I have something for you."

"What is it?"

Reggie produces a cell phone and hands it to Mac. "Hello" he says in anguish. "Yup."

He hands the phone back to Reggie and says, "Get me outta here."

CHAPTER 6

THE LIFT

The crew has been made aware of the target; the plans have been drawn...let the games begin.

It is the night of the much-anticipated unveiling of a rare piece of art at the Boston Museum of Science—a painting called L'Angelo di Ragusa (in English: The Angel of Ragusa) dug up beneath the foundation of a construction site in the town of Ragusa, Sicily. The artist, Mario Ardolito, was said to have painted a portrait of a beautiful woman with hair as black as a crow's plumes, eyes sparkling bright and blue, and olive skin so breathtakingly beautiful that the image could only have come from a dream. This woman sits idle on a small dock, dipping her toes in the calm waters of the Mediterranean Sea. The canvas dates back to the 16th century. The price is rumored to be as high as several million dollars, up to $10 million some say.

Jake arrives at the museum fifteen minutes early, but when he's about to cross the street to enter, his attention is drawn to an elderly woman about to unwittingly walk into traffic. So he races over to her and raises his hand up like a traffic cop to halt the oncoming cars. They stop, he takes the woman by the arm and walks her the rest of the way. The ordeal takes him five minutes off-schedule, and in those precious moments, the line to enter the party has tripled in length. There's pressure now, as Jake needs to post up near the painting to clear the way for the take. The woman says, "Boy, I wish I could see what's going on in there tonight."

"Come on, darling," said Jake, "I'll get you in."

The line is moving slowly, like a chain gang in the desert heat, so he keeps her on his arm as they walk to the front. He tells the ticket taker (an elderly gentleman who, based on his expression, would rather be at home watching the evening news) that he needs to get his mother into the party before anyone else so she can grab a seat, as she can't stand for long. The old guy nods and lets them in. Mac, watching all of this from his van, can't help but feel great bewilderment. Nonetheless, Jake is in, and he's on time. He finds the old woman a seat and goes off on his own.

Exactly one hour into the historic evening, the crowd of roughly 150 has dwindled to less than half. Among the remaining is none other than Jake, hiding in plain sight, paying no additional esteem to the artwork, although still standing close enough to absorb its finest details.

Disguised as a waiter in a white coat and black bowtie, pushing a cart with hors d'oeuvres through the vast white corridor, is Chops.

Jake stands still holding a glass of champagne when a woman dressed more for Sunday school than a gala approaches, also holding a glass of champagne. She has a shy way about her and a natural aura, though she possesses a cuteness that's enough to steal a man's attention away for at least a moment. She stands fixed with a strong gaze on the painting until her focus gives way to a voice.

"What do you think?" asked Jake.

She turns to his direction, a bit surprised by the question from a stranger, and says, "Oh, uh, honestly, I'm getting so tired of these works," the woman said. "It's just one artist after another painting the woman of his dreams, because the scores of self-manifested perversions for her weren't enough …she probably fell in love with his best friend or something, never to be seen again."

Jake responds, "Well, that's certainly a bleak perspective, I must say."

"I'm the forever cynic…so I've been told. So what's your assessment, then?"

"I see a tragic love story told through the eyes of the lovesick artist using the finest of strokes and just the right blend of colors to make even a grown man cry," responded Jake.

"That's deep."

"Thank you. Personally, I prefer the artists from London, but that's just me," he said.

Jake's answer brings a grin to the woman's face. She extends her hand and says, "Hi, I'm Amelia."

"I'm Jake."

"So, how long have you lived in the States?" she asked.

"I came over when I was eight."

"Eight?" she asked, surprised. "And you maintained the accent all this time?"

Jake quips, "I heard the ladies find it sexy."

Amelia chuckles, then focuses back on the painting. "And what is it that you do?"

"I'm a longshoreman."

"Really?" Amelia says in a degree of bewilderment. "A longshoreman with an artistic palate…not something you see every day."

"It's a nice escape from the docks," he says. "It can be a rough place."

"I've heard."

Then he asks, "How about yourself? What do you do?"

"I'm a school teacher…kindergarten."

"That's really great."

"It has its moments. Honestly, though," she said, as she fixes her eyes back on the painting, "I'd be remiss if I did not admit that this woman in the painting reminds me of a young Audrey Hepburn…like in the movie 'Funny Face' with Humphrey Bogart."

"Fred Astaire."

"Sorry?"

"She was in Funny Face," said Jake, "opposite Fred Astaire. It was the movie 'Sabrina' that she starred in with Bogart."

"You know your movies, I'm impressed."

"I know my classics. And you know your paintings."

Amelia says, "Only the peculiar ones."

Jake looks at his watch and draws a curious look from Amelia.

"Have another engagement?" she asked.

"No, I'm sorry, I didn't mean to be rude."

"It's OK, you can only look at a still object for so long, however interesting it is."

"It depends how beautiful that object is."

Amelia blushes.

Just then, Chops maneuvers closer, to the base of the painting. Jake places his right hand against Amelia's waist and helps guide her a half-step to her left to make room for Chops and the cart to get by. At the precise moment that Amelia plants her feet, the room goes pitch dark. The lights have gone out, causing a few murmurs and gasps from the small crowd. But not Jake. He draws Amelia closer to him in a near embrace and whispers to her, "It's OK."

There is a faint click-clack sound from nearby, and then another one. After roughly two whole minutes, the lights return, and everything is as it was. No one moves, not even Chops. He stands as most are with a curious expression before he shrugs his shoulders and wheels the cart away into the banquet kitchen.

"Well," says Amelia, "I guess that's my cue." She reaches into her purse, retrieves a business card, and hands it to Jake. "I'm usually not this forward, but it's been a real pleasure meeting you. Give me a call some time."

"A teacher with a business card?"

"I also tutor on weekends."

"I didn't mean any disrespect," he said.

"I never felt that for a second."

"I see. So, was it the accent?" asked Jake.

"You betcha."

She walks off toward the exit. Jake takes a strong look at the painting, then smiles because he knows it's a fake, and that Chops has wheeled away the real one.

CHAPTER 7

HOW THEY DID IT

The morning of the heist, Robby had visited the museum and immersed himself in any and all displays in front of him, so long as a member of the security staff was close by. He approached an animal exhibit housing what appeared to be an adult bear and cub behind a wide glass enclosure. While gazing at the displays, he gently placed his palms on the glass, causing the guard to look in his direction. "Sir, please do not touch the glass," a voice called out. But Robby paid no mind and began knocking on the glass as if he were trying to get the bear's attention. The antic brought the attention of the guard instead, and he walked briskly over to Robby. But Robby kept at it to provoke the guard into getting close, as was the case when he grabbed Robby's knocking hand and lowered it forcefully. The guard's nostrils flared and eyebrows wrinkled when he said, "That's enough!"

It worked. Robby got the guard close enough to swipe his ID badge and keys dangling from his belt.

One week before the robbery, Chops surveilled the catering company, Pro Service Catering. His goal: To learn when they had their uniforms dry-cleaned, and who was in charge of the operation on any given day. The business itself was an undersized warehouse nestled in the middle of a dozen or so outlets and department stores. It was used for two things only: As a home base for hiring service workers, and for the purposes of housing and distributing uniforms to said workers. Most days, there would be two managers handling the operation because that's all it took to make a hiring decision and hand out a white blazer and bowtie.

After Chops' reconnaissance, he had set up an interview with a hiring manager named Fred Rollins, whom he had learned drove a green Toyota Prius that he naturally parked right outside in a packed consumer lot.

Chops had set up the interview perfectly to coincide with the uniform manager's lunch break, and the decision to do so worked out well. So Chops walked and headed right for the only person in the place, Fred, who was sitting behind a desk and shuffling paperwork. He was short and round with a greasy bald scalp, clad in grey sweatpants and a Boston Bruins hockey Jersey with #30 on the back. Chops came in carrying a suit bag over his shoulder, on which Fred immediately remarked, "Do you always take your dry cleaning around with you?"

"Oh, this?" Chops said, removing it from his backside. "No, sorry, it's funny…or not funny, actually, but I just saw someone outside trying to get into a green Prius. And since this is my favorite suit, I thought I'd bring it in with me."

Fred's eyes widened in terror. He said, "Did you say a green Prius?"

"Yes. Is that yours?"

"Hang on," said Fred frantically as he bolted around his desk and headed for the exit. Once he disappeared, Chops beelined it for the uniforms and began to search quickly for his size. Done. He grabbed one, and then dipped his hand in a pile of nametags meant for current employees. He swiftly pulled one out and pocketed it, then placed the jacket in the suit bag while walking back to Fred's desk. As soon as he sat back, Fred re-entered. He said, "Looks like nothing was missing…maybe the person just ran off."

"Fantastic."

Mac's approach was less fluent compared to the others when it came to completing his role for the job. He pulled the fire alarm.

Using the museum security guard's badge and dressed like a blue collar worker of sorts, Mac slipped into the control room of the museum and wired everything up to his receiver—everything from the lights to the inferred laser alarms were now under his control. Once he was satisfied, he turned off the alarm on his own, locked the front door electronically, walked to the back of the museum, to the service elevator, down to the ground floor and out an exit, undetected.

As soon as he was off the property, he reopened the front door to allow the fire department to search for the cause of the alarm.

Jake, well, was the quarterback of the operation. He planned it, oversaw each detail, and made sure the painting and the area surrounding it was crystal clear. Most importantly, though, he stole the replica painting that Chops put back up during the take.

It was bound for a warehouse on Huntington Avenue in Boston. But before it was in transit, it needed to be offloaded from a ship and onto the docks, passing right through Jake's hands. So, as Jake and his work gang unloaded the ship, he held his box aside and marked it up conspicuously so when he went back to pick it up, he'd have no doubt it was the right one. And so he did. He carved the letters "ITP" meaning "Italian painting" and left the box tucked away in the corner of the cargo hold. He later went back, scooped it up, and walked off the ship without anyone paying him any mind, especially his fellow longshoremen.

The duplicate was a means to an end, not an actual score, so taking it did not break Jake's self-imposed rule of taking anything off the docks.

And that is how it they did it.

CHAPTER 8

WHO THEY DID IT FOR

His name is Nicola D'Agostino, or Nick. He's a Boston native who as a child chummed around with young Gussy back in the old West End of Boston. And while Gussy found his way onto the docks as a longshoreman, Nick made a fortune by first high jacking trucks, any trucks, as long as they were hauling something of value; meaning items he could move easily on the street. With the help of his small three-man crew, he once took a National Foods truck packed with a grocery store-style load, and fenced the entire haul systematically to a dozen restaurants in Boston's North End.

Though taking food off trucks was among the more stress-free operations, gold, diamonds, and straight cash was something else. But as risky as it was having to incapacitate a few guards, or worse, put a few bullets in them or get shot at himself, the payoff in Nick's mind always outweighed the dangers.

Over time he developed connections all over the world, and he had to in order to find the right individuals who could act as buyers for the rare items he took, or launderers for the cash. And thanks to Gussy, he had a local one named Joe "Honk" Augusta. Honk got his nickname as a result of his musical prowess, especially his talent for playing the saxophone. He and Gussy were close; in fact, when Honk's family came over from Gaeta, Italy, Gussy's parents sponsored Honk's family and helped them through the transition of relocating to America. He often tells Gussy he's forever indebted to him. As far as his relationship with Nick, it was strictly business. Call it a professional rivalry, but for whatever reason, the two never admired one another.

So Nick became a multimillionaire, and as the cash flowed in, so did his need for protection. He cozied up with the right people, including judges and politicians, and all the while nestled in the good graces of each and every Boston neighborhood by donating what he could to a number of charitable causes: Local boys' and girls' clubs, churches, and homeless shelters were among his favorites.

Today Nick has a new subordinate, and his name is Jake. Naturally it was Gussy who put the two together when he first approached his son and said, "Listen, if you're going to go all in with this thing, taking all the big stuff, you're going to need someone who can unload it for you, someone we can both trust, and that someone is Nick." Jake accepted the offer and solidified his operation with added protection and a way to unload the goods more seamlessly through his Pop's friend. The only drawback is that Nick will now take a cut. Still, in Jake's eyes, it was all worth it.

He began working with Nick alone before he met Chops, Robby, and Mac. However, after years of turning hard work and continuous risk into reward, Jake has finally seen the light at the end of the tunnel.

CHAPTER 9

LIFE IS GOOD

Jake had a plan to follow the "Italian heist," and it was to quit the docks, isolate himself, buy a boat and enjoy life the way he'd intended when he began his career as a successful thief. But not all plans work out, and when he picked up the phone and dialed Amelia's number, his life would never be the same.

The pair immediately began seeing each other, and over the course of several months developed a strong, intimate, and committed relationship. It was time for Jake to escape the waywardness of his past and embark on a new life with a new woman. But for Jake, that meant letting Amelia in, to let her know and understand him and where he came from.

On a leisurely stroll through the Boston Commons Jake began to open up, but only when provoked.

Amelia says, "So, Mr. Classic Movies, you know all the details of my life, as boring as they are. I unabashedly told you all about my sheltered life, from my days as a ballerina to the moment I quit playing the trombone in the high school band."

"What are you getting at, exactly?" Jake asked with a crooked smile.

"I want to know what happened to your parents," said Amelia. "I know you said they passed, but how? And if you don't want to talk about it, it's OK. I'm usually not this bold, but I really want to know you."

"No, no," Jake insisted. "You deserve to know." He went on, "They were murdered."

"Oh my God, I'm so sorry."

"It's OK," he said, "it was 1983...my dad decided to take my ma and I to a department store in London called Harrods. We were going to pick out something nice for her. She'd just finished nursing school, and my dad wanted to give her something nice. I remember being so excited that he let me have a say in what he bought. Ultimately, though, it was my ma who decided on a bracelet that we picked out. My dad had just paid for it when my ma reached in the bag and put the bracelet on. Then it happened."

"What happened?"

"A bomb exploded in the store. It went off and knocked me off my feet. In an instant, the store had become rubble beneath a cloud of smoke and dust. When I regained my footing, I walked gingerly to avoid stepping on something or someone. I was looking for my parents. There they were...they were both lying on the floor, holding hands. But they were gone. My ma still had the bracelet on."

Amelia's eyes welled up and she placed her hand atop his.

"Next thing I knew, I was in the hospital. I had only minor cuts and bruises, so I was discharged a day later to the care of my neighbor, William." Jake went on, "A few days later we buried my parents. I left my ma's bracelet on her. A day later I got up and ran and just kept running until I saw the waterfront, and I continued and raced to a ship and up its gangway. I had no idea where it was going, I just knew I couldn't stay in London. A week later is when Gussy found me, right here in Boston where the ship docked."

"Did you ever go back?"

"I did," said Jake, "after I finished high school I went to London to get more answers, and I did. But there wasn't much to learn. I got the closure I wanted, I guess, then decided to join Her Majesty's Army...I served in the UKSF...the Special Forces. Foolishly, I thought I could exact some revenge on those who murdered my parents, but instead I got sent to the Middle East and did four tours there. I learned a lot in the bush, and I loved my team, but I really felt more at home back in Boston with Gussy, ya know?"

"I do," she said.

"I owe that guy everything. So anyway, I came back several years later. That's when he got me the job on the docks."

"So what does it mean to be a United Kingdom Special Forces soldier?" she asked. "What kinds of things did you learn?"

"Lots of things," he said, "like counter-terrorism, special-reconnaissance..."

"Did you have a favorite?" she said. "And stop me if I'm asking too many questions."

"No, it's OK. You want to know me," he said. "Don't worry, I'll have my turn."

She smiles.

Jake said, "I felt more in my element when the command came down for DA, or Direct Action. Those were small-scale raids, ambushes, things like that."

"Sounds exciting, but so dangerous."

"It was both. Some of it, quite honestly, I'd like to forget."

"Thank you for telling me all of that," said Amelia. "I mean everything. I'm sure it's not something you divulge often."

"It's not. And thank you for listening."

"It's what I'm here for. And by the way, this is for you," she said as she handed him a necklace with a locket dangling from it.

Jake takes it. He's visibly moved and says, "You didn't have to do this."

"I know," she said, "I wanted to. Open it."

Jake opens the silver dollar-sized locket to see a picture of the two of them in a warm embrace. "It's beautiful," said Jake, as he placed it around his neck. "No one's ever given me anything like this."

"Well, I'm glad I'm the first to do so."

CHAPTER 10

ONLOOKER

It had been just six months since "The Angel" had been taken and, true to Jake's ambitions, the gang had split up and gone their separate ways until further notice. During such time, Jake left the docks and is enjoying an early retirement, but he wasn't alone. He and Amelia are now embarking on a thriving courtship that saw the two nearly inseparable and gaining steam with every passing day. And though she's still maintaining her employment as a teacher, she wouldn't miss the opportunity to be with Jake on his boat's maiden voyage. Thus Amelia took the month of April off in preparation of sailing down the East Coast together to Miami, where they would dock his brand new

35-foot Carver 396 Motor Yacht. It was long, glistening and white, with blue trim, tinted windows, and an expansive living quarters down below.

After making a few stops along the way including Baltimore, the Outer Banks of North Carolina, and Savannah, GA., the William Madeline (so named after Jake's late parents), dropped anchor at the Miami Beach Marina.

It's the second week of April, and already the heat and humidity have become unforgiving, and the rains hammering at times, but the couple cares little, especially Amelia, who enthusiastically suggested they choose Miami as the destination because she's never been.

So, there they are lunching at a seaside bistro when Amelia admits she's become a bit tired and prefers a nap in the boat to anything else. Jake decides to go for a walk and look for a spot to have a drink before he returns to the William Madeline. But he notices a gentleman sitting at a table with only a drink in front of him. Hardly extraordinary at a coastal restaurant in South Florida, but to Jake, something feels a bit offbeat. The man is well-dressed with dark sunglasses, long, oily hair and a noticeable habit of peering over at Jake every few minutes.

Jake signs for the check and says, "Are you sure you're going to be OK?"

"Of course, babe," she said. "Go for a walk, I'll meet you back at the boat, I'm just really tired."

They stand and kiss before leaving together, then split at the exit. Jake walks along South Miami Avenue, passing the cafés and vibrant outdoor bars. He pauses to light up a cigarette and leans on the stone wall to face the ocean. He looks to his right to see the man from the restaurant roughly 30 meters away and posing the same way. So Jake walks again and into a more crowded area, and the man follows him two more blocks into a gift shop.

Jake is a street guy with a staunch military mind, and he knows all-too-well the footfalls of a man that simply do not seem right. For Jake, this man was easy to make, but a man to take seriously.

And so the mysterious man waits outside until a few minutes later when Jake appears. He continues on his unplanned path threading his way through a host of people until he makes a sudden move and enters a bar, a high-end cigar lounge called Casa de Montecristo and among the most popular stomping grounds for Miami's elite. Jake takes a seat at the bar and orders a bourbon on the rocks. As the bartender places the drink in front of him, the mysterious fella casually sits on the stool directly to Jake's right.

"You've been following me," Jake said.

"Yes, I have," the suspicious character said in broken English. "I'll be brief. I was hoping you would consider meeting my boss, he's a great fan of your work, and would like to offer you an opportunity. He'll pay you handsomely, of course."

All the while, neither man turn to look at each other. Jake in fact never responds to him.

"My name is Hector, everything else you need to know is here," he said as he slides over a small folded white piece of paper in front of Jake and says, "including the time and place." Hector turns away and leaves. Jake opens the paper to read a handwritten note:

2pm tomorrow – The Coco Hough Club
Look for the man in the white coat

About an hour passes when Jake returns to the boat and inspects the vessel feverishly, but not looking for a blemish, but to secure the area in case of any unwanted presence lurking. There were none, but Hector now has his attention, as well as anyone who so much as looks at him or Amelia the wrong way. His curiosity catches the eye of Amelia, who emerges from below deck. "Is everything OK, honey?" she asked.

"Of course, why wouldn't it be?"

"You seem a little too focused, on edge even."

"Old habits, darling," he said with a slightly slanted grin.

"Well, try to relax, we're in paradise," said Amelia. "Why don't you come down here and inspect *me*."

"Oh, yeah?"

"Yeah," she says turning slowly and seductively, but leaving her eyes on Jake. She walks back down below, maintaining eye contact. Jake takes the bait, follows her down below, and closes the door behind him.

CHAPTER 11

A SIMPLE OFFER

The Coco Hough Club. It's a dimly lit, smoky, private lounge carved out from the basement of an unassuming laundromat on Collins Avenue, just off Ocean Boulevard. The walls boasted pictures of legendary characters from Al Capone to Dean Martin and Winston Churchill. In the back corner rested a private, round table reserved for Miami's highest of societal figures including politicians, judges, and even local gangsters. Today that corner harbored Carlos Esteban, an established hood in South Florida with ties to Cuba and its lucrative drug trade. He was tall and thin with jet-black hair thrown back and clad in a pricy black suit, with his stingy-brim fedora resting on the table to his right. His third whiskey was nearly consumed; his cigar was a burning perfection. That's when his guest arrived, and it was Jake. He stood at the edge of the table before Carlos, and it was obvious he was being sized up. The moment ended when Carlos politely asked him to sit down.

"I see Hector finally got something right. He's not completely useless after all," said Carlos, provoking a collective chuckle from the pair of bodyguards stationed side-by-side a few feet away from Jake's backside.

"What is it that you want?" said Jake, unamused.

"I heard about you," said Carlos. "You fought, scraped, and clawed your way through the streets to survive and become something. And this, all after you lost your parents in that terrible accident. I, too, was born less fortunate, in Cuba, in fact. I had to do things that would give most men nightmares, and I had to do them as a boy, I had to do them to survive."

Jake sits idle, unmoved by Carlos' tales of heroism.

After a moment, Carlos reacts to Jake's posture, "Yes, yes, let's get down to business. We're busy men, and I can appreciate that," he went on after he took a swig of his whiskey, finishing what's left. "I understand you're a man who can...get things."

"I don't know what you heard, but I'm just a part-time dock worker and a veteran of Your Majesty's Royal Army."

"Listen to me very carefully. I'm not in the business of wasting time, I know what you do, and I need you to do it for me, just once. It is a simple offer."

"You're too late," said Jake.

"I'm sorry?"

Jake said, "I don't have a crew anymore, we've gone our separate ways."

"That's unfortunate," Carlos went on, "but maybe I can tempt you and your crew with a good faith offer, let's say a $5 million dollar cash advance, then $5 million dollars after you complete the job? Will that bring them back together?"

"No."

"What if I had a crew already you could work with?" asked Carlos.

Jake dismissively grins at the suggestion.

"We're talking about a lot of money here, Jake," said Carlos.

Jake asks, "What in God's name is so valuable that you're willing to pay so much for it?"

"That, my friend, is information available only when the agreement is struck." Carlos went on, "Do we have a contract, Mr. Jake?"

"I don't know you, and I don't know what you want so badly, so I'm going to have to say no."

"You say no?"

"That's right. I'm sorry."

That doesn't sit well with Carlos, and his still, blank and unabbreviated gaze is evidence of that. After a few moments he breaks his stare and says, "I'm sorry, too. You can go."

Jake stands, politely nods, turns and walks between the bodyguards, then out the door and into the blazing sunlight.

CHAPTER 12

THE NAB

Only hours have passed since his encounter with Carlos, and in that time, Jake felt it necessary to make contact with Boston, more specifically, Nick.

From a payphone, Jake says, "…he seems to know a lot about me. His name is Carlos Esteban, Cuban thug in Miami…we could fill Fenway Park with the likes of that profile, I know, but what do you have on this guy, if anything?"

"His name doesn't ring a bell," said Nick. "I'm sorry. I can send a couple of guys down there if you like for added protection, just say the word. In the meantime, I'll do some digging to see what he's really about."

"No, don't send anyone. I'm leaving this place soon, but thanks for the offer."

"I'm sorry I couldn't help you further, my boy," said Nick. "Miami is a world of its own, and if you're not careful, it could be the last place you ever see. You were right to turn him down, kid. You don't know him, it's best to walk away."

"Thanks, Nick."

"You got it, kid," he said. "By the way, do you know your pops is? Been trying to get a hold of him, but can't reach him."

"Yeah, sorry, Nick, my old man met a broad as it turns out, and she's got him traveling all over the place. I think he's in Naples, Italy, right now. He'll be back in a few weeks."

"OK, kid, thanks. Listen, you take care of yourself."

"I will. You, too, Nick."

"See ya, kid."

Amelia is kept in the dark about the day's events, while Jake now moves about with an air of caution.

That same day, within the hour the sun had set on Miami, Jake raises the question to Amelia: "What if we left Miami and took a trip to the Caribbean and checked out some of the islands?" he asks. "We'll stay at a nice place right on the water."

Amelia responds, "That sounds like a wonderful idea, babe, but just a few more days here, OK? I've almost had my fill."

Jake reluctantly says, "Sure, sweetheart, we can do that."

So they stay, and for the remaining time, Jake clings to her side, but Amelia is feisty and at times even demands some privacy as she takes in the attractions.

Two days since the meeting, and with no noticeable tails since then, Jake begins to loosen his grip on his protection of Amelia and starts to enjoy himself.

It's the eve of their last scheduled day in Miami, the pair head to a popular nightclub just off the strip called Blackbird Ordinary. It's a place known to teem with rambunctious partygoers, professional athletes, actors and musicians. This night is no different. They can see all from the privacy of their own booth that Jake reserved and watch as members of the Miami Dolphins file in along with acting legend Sylvester Stallone, towing a small crowd likely to be his entourage.

After a couple of hours of sipping martinis and occasional dancing, the couple pays the tab and heads out. A mere 20 minutes elapses before they're back on the boat, changed and in bed. During the wee hours of the night, Amelia gets out of bed, prompting Jake to open his eyes momentarily.

"I just need some air," said Amelia.

Jake nods and dozes off. Shortly thereafter, the boat is rocked by a loud thump, thunderous enough to wake Jake fully this time. He fixes his eyes and props himself up and notices Amelia has not come back, so he immediately leaps out of bed and heads for the deck. He circles the boat and calls her name, but there's no response, no sign of her. Scouring the deck with a flashlight now, and after careful examination, the scene was clear: no blood and no visible damage to any structure. What he does notice is that a pair of her walking shoes is now missing. *Perhaps she left something back at the club and went to retrieve it*, he thinks to himself. *Then why the loud bang?*

Dawn approaches, and Jake has left the confines of the William Madeline and begins patrolling on shore. He treks on quickly but carefully, popping his head in and out of every sunglass stand, souvenir store, café, and bar, but the few places open at this early hour are mostly devoid of patrons. As he searches, he periodically calls her cell phone and leaves a message each time telling her he's concerned.

He scans the beach, and it's scarce enough of people that if he saw her, he could identify her. But she is nowhere.

As he takes a breather in the brutal morning-time humidity of South Florida, his cell phone rings. He jams his hand quickly into his pocket and pulls it out.

He answers, "Hello!"

A deep and surly voice responds, "We have your girl."

"Who is this?"

"You know."

It's not Carlos, but whoever it is, he's being ordered by him.

"OK," says Jake. "I know. So where is she?"

"You know how this works," the voice says. "You do for us, we do for you."

"All this over what, a fucking painting?"

"Who said anything about a painting?"

"Then what is it?" Jake asks.

"You know the rules. The answer you're looking for is on a need-to-know basis, and right now, you need to concentrate on getting your little band of thieves together, and then you'll get the mark. And if everything goes as planned, you and sweetie pie will be together again. But you take one misstep, and you'll get her back in pieces."

"How do I know she's alive now?"

"Jake!" cries out Amelia in distress from the other end of the line.

"Satisfied?"

"You know what I'll do to you if you hurt her. You know what I'm capable of," says Jake.

"It's funny, they all say that, but in the end…well, I don't have to tell you. Wait for a call. It will come this Saturday at 5:00 p.m."

The person ends the call. Jake realizes that if he does not comply with Carlos' demands, they may very well kill Amelia, and all because she was with him. His past has always haunted him, and now it has grabbed hold of her, that is certain. He couldn't save his parents as a child, but he can save Amelia as a man, and so he goes to work.

CHAPTER 13

ALDEN FREEMAN AND THE DAGGER

Jake is back at The Coco Hough Club. He calmly makes his way to where Carlos is sitting and, not surprisingly, he's accompanied by a pair of bodyguards. One extends his arm across Jake's chest and says, "Arms out." So Jake spreads 'em while he's patted down. "He's clean."

"Please, sit, Jake," Carlos says. "I want this to be pleasant for both of us."

Jake takes a seat cautiously.

"I'm sorry, Jake, that it had to be this way," begins Carlos.

"You know if you hurt her…"

"I know full well what your intentions would be, Jake," says Carlos, "I can assure you she is in good health, and is being taken care with much attentiveness…for now. Let's get down to business, shall we?"

Jake nods while his teeth are clenched, his expression steadfast and stone-faced.

Carlos says, "I want something, Jake. Something so wonderful, so beautiful, and so priceless, I will do anything to have it. Absolutely anything."

"Tell me what it is," says Jake.

"It is a dagger, Jake. An ancient relic that once belonged to the Queen of Castile, Queen Isabella of Spain. As a way of showing gratitude, she gifted this dagger to Christopher Columbus just before his first voyage to the New World. And he carried it everywhere with him from Europe to the New World, and everyplace thereafter. Columbus before his death passed it on to his son, Diego, where it remained in Alcazar De Colon (a house in Santo Domingo and built by Diego himself) for centuries."

"So where's this dagger now?" asks Jake.

"It's right here in Miami."

"Where?"

"A man named Alden Freeman, an architect and very wealthy man, had quite an affinity for all things antiquated. In fact, this man was actually a descendant of the Mayflower. Alden Freeman once made the same trip to Alcazar De Colon, and during his time there he was offered to design an estate so big, so magnificent for the soon-to-be dictator Rafael Trujillo, but Freeman declined the initial offer, which was a large sum of money. Instead, he offered his design to Trujillo under the condition that he could receive the dagger as payment. Freeman insisted the dagger was so well guarded that not even Trujillo could procure the treasure for him. But it was Freeman who played his tricks on Trujillo with his words, forcing him to prove his strength with his reverse psychology. Trujillo took the bait and demanded the dagger from the Alcazar De Colon using the threat of death. And his tactic proved successful. The Alcazar De Colon gave up the dagger without a fight. Trujillo got his home, and Freeman, the dagger."

Quietly but impatiently, Jake says, "Why are you telling me all this?"

"Credibility, you see." Carlos goes on. "Anyone can tell a good story, but with no evidence to back up its claims, it becomes nothing but a fairytale. I have that evidence," says Carlos as he slowly reaches in his inside suit pocket to reveal an old, tattered pocketbook and lays it on the table. "I have Alden Freeman's diary," he says, "and in it he speaks of the dagger, his love for it, and where it is located today. In his last entry in 1937 he says, 'I leave you to our home, our villa, but I will see you again.' The villa he speaks of is the Villa, Casa Casuarina. You know it as the Versace Mansion. And every night, he

64

says in this diary, he would visit the dagger in its resting place and stare at it for hours on end before he retired to bed. You see, even at the hour of his death, he admits here that the dagger was in his possession, and 'til this day it remains in the mansion, guarded by a woman, a woman of great beauty I presume, but I do not know who or what that means."

"We're not archeologists, we don't hunt for treasure. We mark it and take it."

"And I am not a kidnapper," says Carlos. "You see, I am just a man with a purpose. And now, so are you. Find that secret hiding place, bring me the dagger, and once I compare it to the diagram in this diary you will be reunited with your love."

"How did you come across this diary, I wonder?" asks Jake.

"Some things are better left unsaid," Carlos says. "I've told you everything you need to know. You have one week. And please, Jake, don't try anything stupid. Bring me the real dagger."

"Likewise," said Jake.

On the surface, all signs and expressions on display depict Carlos as the one who holds all the cards, who has nothing to lose, and does his best to show off his bravado in front of Jake. But the tension is palpable. A careful observer might even see that the one who truly lacks fear, the one who should be feared, is Jake. While Carlos might boast he's tangled with some of the more unsavory characters in his underworld, his body language suggests he's been profoundly affected by Jake's coldness and calmness, and perhaps he's never encountered anyone of Jake's ilk.

"Good day," said Carlos.

With that, Jake stands, nods, and walks out of the Club.

CHAPTER 14

THE GANG IS BACK

Immediately following Jake's second meeting with Carlos, one by one, he signals a member of the crew the old-fashioned way, at a payphone. He knows Carlos will do his utmost to track his whereabouts at all times, as well as all of his communications; in essence, keep tabs on his progress until the job is completed. But Jake is good. Not only did he lose Carlos' insignificant tails, he was able to tail them back to where Carlos spent most of his days, in his yacht at the marina.

Chops becomes the first to be reached. He's nearing the end of the spring semester and preparing final exams, but he happily puts it all on the back burner to come to the aid of his friend. But his workload and responsibilities matter little, as Chops can come and go as he pleases given his leverage over the school's top leadership. Jake receives similar love from Mac, who recently found employment with a racing crew and is actually close by at the Daytona International Speedway. Instead of lamenting another loss with his team and catching a bus to the next race, he jumps in his white van with all of his technical equipment packed in and heads straight for South Beach. And Robby, who's in the middle of a high-stakes poker game in Las Vegas, answers the call, much to the dismay of the other players, leaves the game, and heads straight to the airport.

Jake never forgot the words Gussy had embedded in his brain when it came to stealing. He said if you have confidence, poise, and purpose, you can get away with anything. But it's loyalty that makes up a great team, loyalty from everyone. And that's what Jake had; the respect and loyalty of his crew.

Next he dials Nick, hoping he had the opportunity to take him up on the offer of sending a couple of guys down to assist and/or protect. But this time he's having trouble connecting with him, and since time is of the essence, he focuses his attention on the task at hand: learning the target, extracting it, and saving Amelia.

Jake and the other three meet at the Miami Hostel on Alton Road just three days after Amelia was taken. It's a

Saturday, and by now Jake has already procured a copy of the original blueprints of the Villa, Casa Casuarina, the ones drawn up by Alden Freeman himself, as well as the current ones created for the design of the hotel structure standing today. And he found them both at the Miami Public Library in the digital archives, available to print. Each copy was much smaller, naturally, than the originals (16x10 to be exact), but it was all he would need.

Each member of the crew all admit they're doing well, and so they sit down on the beds while Jake briefs them on what he knows. "Gentlemen," he begins, "we're going to rob the Versace Mansion."

Its beauty is vast, colorful and picturesque. The estate is protected by an impressive wall of lush greenery with tall, relentlessly manicured bushes, masterfully sculptured statues, and an unwavering amount of foot traffic from tourists and locals alike looking to catch a glimpse of the most famous mansion in South Beach, Miami, and one of the most iconic in the world.

But it's the secrets that the mansion holds: throughout the lavish fortress are several doorways covered up by renovations over the decades. Even though it had been home to Alden Freeman, the property was originally constructed as an apartment building, so to transform the complex from that to a mansion and back to a hotel undoubtedly took many cosmetic and necessary structural overhauls. When all was said and done, it was one of the most stunning, elegant, and admired Italian-influenced edifices in the world, protecting a mysterious relic ready to be rediscovered.

The others offer little reaction when told of the mark, as like a well-trained military unit, the target is the target. So Jake lays out the plans side-by-side, and begins to point out the differences and similarities, and he cautions, "This Alden Freeman was a clever and cunning architect, and if what Carlos is saying is true, this thing is well hidden, somewhere between this," Jake points to a tall structure called the Amish Tower (The Tower was built in homage to Christopher Columbus by his son Diego. It was where Columbus was banished. Freeman built a replica, and it's remained untouched for nearly 100 years), then runs his finger down the plans to the front of the mansion near the front gates. "And this," he said, "while most of the mansion has gone through a number of physical changes, this area I've just shown you has barely been touched, which is why I believe the secret lies somewhere in between the two spots I pointed out. Now, this woman he mentioned, the so-called guardian of the treasure, could be anything; a painting, a bust, a statue, or simply a name spelled out on a wall or object. What this means is we'll need to be diligent. Nonetheless, given what we know and the clues I've received, I truly believe that half the battle has been won."

"What's this treasure we're looking for, boss?" asked Robby.

"It's a dagger, the one shown here," Jake draws a piece of paper from his back pocket; it's a page torn from an encyclopedia showing a picture of each side of the dagger taken in 1929, as stated below the photograph. He unfolds it and lays it on the bed. The other three lean in for a closer look and can see that its blade shines brightly, and its handle is remarkably detailed with an inscription that wraps around it and reads, "*Deja que esta daga sea tu guia para laequidad y la justicia end nuestro Nuevo Mundo.*" In English it's translated as, "Let this dagger be your guide to fairness and justice in our New World."

Jake says, "Again, using what we know, and keeping these plans to memory, I think we'll be OK. We will, in fact, have to reserve a room at the mansion, so we're allowed access to all of the common areas...you never know where we'll find a clue. Once we we've located it, we'll move at night and take it. Understood?"

"Yes," the others says collectively.

"Good," says Jake, "Lastly, "only one will check into the mansion, and that is Chops. There's not much more we can discuss at this point, given the time we have," Jake states.

With that, Jake pillars his arms on the table and a look of despair washes over his face, which prompts Robby to say, "It's going to be OK," as he places a hand on Jake's shoulder as a show of support.

"I'm sorry, fellas, I really am," says Jake, for getting you all involved, but…

"Don't be like that, boss," says Mac.

"Don't ever say that again," responds Robby.

"We're all in this together," says Chops.

Jake nods to acknowledges the support.

"I do know that Carlos has a yacht down at the marina called the San Luis, or something. Whether or not Amelia is there…that part I don't know," says Jake.

Robby asks, "What if we go after the yacht first and find out if she's there?"

"Because," Jake says, "if Carlos suspects at all that we're not throwing straight dice, he may just kill her, and we'll be too late. Let's play by their rules until that's no longer an option."

"Got it," says Robby.

"Mac, use Darth and go ahead and do your thing and get into the hotel's system…"

Chops interjects when he cups his right hand to his mouth and, in his best Darth Vader voice, says, "Luke, I am your father."

"Knock it off," says Jake. "Mac, make that reservation for three days from now, one night only." He goes on, "Beginning at this moment, there's no time to waste. In a few days, hopefully my life will be restored, and I can forget this shit ever took place."

"Let's do this," says Chops.

Mac unzips his backpack and removes a small laptop from it. He asks, "OK, Chops, what name will you be going by on the reservation? Let's go with something inconspicuous."

"Bruce Wayne, please."

"Bruce Wayne?" asks Mac, who's taken aback. "You call using Batman inconspicuous?"

"Says the guy who named his little gadget Darth Henry," Chops shoots back.

"You don't see me checking into a hotel as Darth Henry, now do you?" Mac says. "What other names you got, Captain America?"

"I left my Steve Rogers I.D. at home."

"Guys! Please!" shouts Jake. "Just pick a name, come on!"

"Bruce Wayne it is," says Mac, as punches the keypad.

CHAPTER 15

CHECKING IN

The following two days were spent on a detailed reconnaissance mission in and around the hotel. Everyone needed to be accounted for, from the bellhop and security guards to the pool cleaners and housekeepers. The operation, as it turned out, was not particularly sophisticated. The hotel has only 10 suites, so it required very little staff, which included just one security officer, bellman, concierge, two front-desk personnel, and a maintenance technician. Only on occasion would the property beef up its employee count, as for: A private party, or if a special guest arrives like a politician or foreign dignitary. Otherwise, on most days, it was pretty quiet, aside from the random guided group tour of the mansion organized by an outside company.

So Chops arrives at the hotel at 3:00 p.m. on the nose. He's clad in light attire including shorts, a polo shirt, and flip flops, although he still has a refined way about him as he patrols the lobby on his way to checking in. A bellman approaches and asks if he can help with his belongings, but Chops carries only an overnight bag and waves him off. Now he does his thing as he carefully absorbs his surroundings and sees that the concierge is idle and ready to handle a guest's query; the maintenance staff member engages in some banter with the housekeeper as they wait for the elevator. The mansion has a laid-back atmosphere about it, much like many other hotels, except this one, on any given day, you could see society's richest and most famous walking about. And it could happen in a blink of an eye. So in a place that once entertained Princess Diana and Madonna, one must prepare for the mansion being turned upside down to accommodate such guests.

It's time to check in. Behind the long-extended marble-covered counter are two very attractive, dark-haired Latina ladies in their mid-to-late twenties. Chops holds his stance before moseying over and watching the women and their trivial movements. The one the left seems ready for anything, not missing a chance to acknowledge a guest through eye contact, a wave, or a nod. She's focused. She's high-energy. The other is trying her best, but periodically takes a glance at her watch while painfully contriving a grin to play the part of an employee overly eager to be of assistance. She looks into space more than once, so one can only deduce she's either flighty or her shift is ending soon. Either way, she's the one.

So Chops approaches her and with a wide smile says, "Hello, I'm here to check in."

Sarah, or so her nametag reads, says, "I'd be happy to help you with that, sir. Can I have an I.D., please?"

"Most certainly," says Chops. He reaches in his pocket and takes out a driver's license and hands it to Sarah.

"Thanks," she responds, and bangs on a few keys on the computer in front of her. "OK, Mr. Wayne," she goes on, "it looks like we have you in the Parrot Suite; it's a beautiful room that was in fact designed in honor of Gianni's niece Allegra, who had a great affinity for birds. Hence the name."

"As do I," says Chops. "But I think you need to check again, because I believe I reserved the Master Suite."

"Oh," says Sarah, "Hmmm, let me take another look." And so she bangs on a few more keys.

Chops looks away and grinds his teeth agitatedly, praying Mac did not mess it up. But there's no mishap, as Sarah suddenly explains, "I'm so sorry, Mr. Wayne, my bad! I looked at the wrong reservation."

But in actuality, the system has turned over at that precise moment right before her eyes. Mac's trick has worked, although the timing was less than ideal.

"It's OK, darling, mistakes happen."

"Great! And can I just get a credit card to match the one I have on file?"

"Of course," answers Chops, before he reaches again in his pocket to retrieve a credit card and hand it to Sarah.

She gives it a close look against what's on her computer screen, then hands it back and says, "Thank you very much, Mr. Wayne. Here is your keycard. Your suite is located on the third floor, and your rate will be $995.00." She goes on, "We won't charge your card until you check out, just in case there's any damage, missing items, or amenities taken advantage of like the minibar or movie rentals. All standard stuff. Is there anything else I can do for you, Mr. Wayne?"

"No, thank you," replies Chops. "You've been very helpful."

Sarah extends her arm and points. "The elevator is right over there."

"Appreciate it."

A moment later, Sarah's attention is once again requested when an up-and-coming hip-hop artist and his entourage of a half-dozen address her. His name is Shifty Lane. "I'm here to check in," he said.

"I'd be happy to help you with that, sir. Can I have an I.D., please?"

Shifty looks back, "Babe, can I have my I.D.?"

A very attractive black woman rolls her eyes as she digs in her purse for the I.D.. She plucks it out and hands it to him. Shifty then hands it to Sabrina.

"OK, Mr. Lane," she goes on, "it looks like we have you in the Parrot Suite; it's a beautiful room that was designed in honor of Gianni's niece Allegra, who had a great affinity for birds…"

"Whoa, girl," Shifty interrupts her, "I'm in the master suite, Gianni Versace's bedroom, that ain't no joke, you need to correct this shit."

Chops catches as much on his walk to the elevator, and smirks as the event unfolds. But the elevator doors close, and he knows it is now Sarah's problem.

CHAPTER 16

TREASURE HUNTING

That evening, at the behest of Jake, the other three branch out into the hotel, specifically to those areas that were a part of the original designs, and comb the property for clues.

"I'll be right behind you," he lets them know. So Robby, Chops, and Mac acquiesce and disburse while Jake remains in the master bedroom alone. His plan is to go through all the pictures Chops had taken in and around the hotel to see if something catches his eye. He studies each down to the tiniest of details. There are a few hundred photos he needs to pore over, and he does so patiently and meticulously. If he sees something that could represent a clue, he circles it.

It's taken hours, but the thick grouping of pictures has been reduced to just eight, each marked with at least one circle indicating an area of importance. Then he examines each of those again, and crosschecks them against the architecture plans. Over and over again he looks for a link between a clue in the photo and what lies next to it, behind it, below it, and so on. The only way to find out is to get an up close and personal look at the real-life figures from the pictures.

It's after midnight now, and the gang is back, and they're exhausted.

"Nothing tonight, boss," says Robby.

"It's OK," says Jake. "Get some rest, we'll hit the pavement early. Except you, Chops. Take a walk with me."

Chops has halfway lowered himself onto a red Cleopatra Fruitwood sofa, then props himself back up unenthusiastically and says, "Yeah."

Jake grabs the pictures and a bottle of water; then he and Chops exit and head for the courtyard.

The courtyard is an open-air, widespread common area where many of the antiquities are visible, including the Amish Tower. It can be an eerie atrium when walking through, as the statues on each side are all facing in and always seem to be looking directly into the eyes of a passerby. They include historical figures such as Confucius, Pocahontas, and Christopher Columbus, of course. There's the massive fountain in the center that it was placed there by the hotel's current owner, Peter Lofton, but undeniably has no significance to the mission at hand.

Jake is thorough, as one would expect, while Chops serves as a second set of eyes and offers another perspective on whatever it is they deem discussion-worthy. But after an hour or so of being dissatisfied with the results, Jake indulges his curiosity while Chops follows outside to the front of the building to the kneeling Aphrodite—Gianni Versace's most treasured piece of art, and set front and center just before the main gates of the hotel. In fact, its beauty is what prompted Versace to purchase the mansion in the first place when he caught a glimpse of it on a leisurely stroll with his sister Donatella.

Jake pauses suddenly, takes a deep breath, and takes in the moment. "Wow," he says.

"Wow, what?" asks Chops.

"It happened right over there," says Jake, pointing to the front steps.

Jake is right, it had happened just a few feet from where the two are standing: it's where the fashion mogul, Gianni Versace, was so callously shot and murdered as he attempted to enter the mansion through the front gates.

It's where his blood had slowly cascaded down the stone steps for all who passed by to see.

"Oh, right," says Chops.

"What do you think, Chops?" says Jake. "Is this our girl?"

"If it is, we're going to have a bitch of a time finding out, I reckon."

So Jake leans on the statue with his right shoulder to check its solidity and sturdiness…she's not moving.

Potted plants make up much of the décor surrounding the statue, but there is one unmistakable feature that Jake can't help but fixate on. It's a metal square box attached to the front of the building and lies to the right of the entrance to the mansion.

It is believed by many, including historians, that the square box is hiding something, a secret, perhaps. The speculation is that it harbors more architecture plans, or even a time capsule left behind by Alden Freeman before he died. No one really knows.

Jake walks over to the box, Chops follows. *What are you hiding in there, I wonder?* Jake thinks to himself. He feels the concrete all around it, and then gives the box a few taps with his knuckles. He then walks around and inside the front entrance and to the right to get on the other side of the mysterious entity, but there's nothing but a wall. To find out what's inside, he'd have to force it open. However, logic would suggest no reason that Freeman would have left the dagger in such close proximity to an entrance that many people used to use to get in, or in such a vulnerable spot where a thief could just smash and grab it.

Jake returns to the front and flags Chops. "Come on, he says, "Let's go, I want to check out that Tower."

As they begin to walk inside, Jake allows a woman to enter first, but she trips, and though she remains upright Jake, always a gentleman, places his hands on each of her arms to give her just a bit of assistance before she thanks him for doing so. Then he notices what she's tripped on; one of the smaller tiles, and said tile has become loose as a result.

So Jake pauses, then bends down and places the tile back in its original spot. He then moves over to Aphrodite and sits at her base, appearing to take a rest.

"We going in?" asks Chops.

"Not yet. Do me a favor and stand next to me and act as a shield in case anyone comes."

Chops obliges.

As carefully and discreetly as possible, Jake takes a small knife from his front pocket, then bends as if he's tying his shoe and begins poking and scraping around one small tile that connects to the base of the statue until he's able to remove it, which happens to be rather easily. Beneath the roughly 3x3" tile is a typical cement backer board often found beneath tile work. What he does next is significant. Jake pours water—enough to cover the space—and watches it closely.

"What are you looking for?" asks Chops.

"It's draining slowly and, come here, take a look at this."

Chops kneels to get a closer look. He sees the remaining water that's waiting to make its way down, and faintly bubbling.

"Whoa," says Chops. "What's that about?"

"It means it's reacting to higher than normal levels of CO_2, which could be the result of poor air quality down below. A condition common in caves when organic material decomposes over a long period of time. And the fact that the water is disappearing means it's found a place to go."

It's you, isn't it? Jake thought to himself, *you're the guardian,* referring to the Kneeling Aphrodite.

Jake covers up the hole with the tile, and heads for the Tower as Chops scurries to catch up.

Since finding his first clue, the idea that the staircase continues on underground is making more sense to him. Jake kneels and pulls out a soft-flamed lighter and places it where the floor meets the last step. There's a subtle, but visible gap between the two, but more importantly, when the flame nears the small space it begins to wave erratically, suggesting there's air coming from below. So he moves behind the staircase where the first flight ascends and he sees that, like several areas of the courtyard, the floor is carpeted. Jake stands, brings his right hand to his chin and begins to size up what he's discovered thus far. Then he gently takes a step forward; one step and he hears a creak in the floor, and it's out of sorts, because nowhere else beneath the carpet will he hear such a thing. His one step brings a smile to his face as he looks down at the carpet.

"Keep your eyes open," he commands Chops.

Again, he takes his knife, and cuts along the edges—just a few inches of each corner—to where the carpet meets the side of the staircase. He pulls it back and sees a piece of plywood roughly 2x2', where a set of tiles would normally be. It's out of place. He wedges his knife along its sides and loosens its hold on the surface beneath. He pauses at times, as people near the curtain. He hears chatter and footsteps, but no one offers a curious look behind him, and if there were, Chops would report it. He lifts the plywood an inch or so using the blade's leverage, then places his fingers between the plywood and cold tiles encasing it and raises it gently. He reveals a hatch with a circular lever. What's more remarkable are the drawings on top of the hatch: Three ships including the Nina, Pinta, and the Santa Maria—the vessels used in Columbus' famous voyage to the New World. After a deep breath, Jake grips the handle and lifts ever so gently, just enough to see it ajar. It's all the evidence he needs.

Their task is complete for now. He heads back to the master bedroom to alert the other two that they've found a way down.

CHAPTER 17

HERE'S THE PLAN

Jake and Chops enter the suite loudly and immediately call to the men, "Wake up, fellas!" Jake called out, "We found it!"

"You found the dagger?" asks Robby as he rubs his eyes to focus.

"Almost. I think it's underground where I thought it might be...but it's below the statue out front," Jake goes on. "Mac, open up Darth."

"You got it," replies Mac, as he retrieves his laptop from his duffle bag.

Jake says, "We need to figure out a way to clear the area in that courtyard for an hour or so, without causing a panic. Any ideas? Here's what I mean. The area I'm talking about is behind the staircase to the Amish Tower. If we're standing right there, we're shielded from anyone hanging around the front of the hotel. But behind us is an open seating area and then the pool." Jake awaits responses with his arms folded, with the expression of a staunch general dialed in and ready to make a plan of attack.

"Fire alarm?" asks Mac.

"Too noisy. Plus, we don't want the fire department combing the hotel while we're trying to work."

"What about a total blackout?" asks Chops.

"No," said Jake. "Well, in theory it's a fine suggestion, but if we have a blackout, we'll need flashlights, and that's enough to raise a lot of suspicion."

"Can I say something, boss?" asks Robby.

"Of course, whatta ya got?"

"Well, let's face it, in a place with only 10 suites, most, if not all are reserved by wealthy individuals, including celebrities in some cases…"

"Like Shifty Lane," Chops interjects.

"Sort of," says Robby dismissively. "My point is, it's not exactly a 'spring break' crowd we have to worry about, it's the staff, and at this time of night, without an extravagant shindig happening, the staff is reduced to a mere five employees: A front desk agent, a security guard, a maintenance guy, bellman, and a room service attendant. If we can draw them all away from the staircase for a fair amount of time, I'm confident we can stave off any guest straggler that might be up at, let's say, 4 a.m.?"

The gang pauses for a moment until Chops says, "How did you know all that?"

"Isn't that what we were supposed to be doing? Recon?"

"Yes, definitely, absolutely," the words shoot out from Chops and Mac.

"It's true," said Jake. "We saw a woman out front, outside, and that was it. We heard a few guests speaking nearby, but we saw no one on the staircase. And by the looks of it, I'll only need a few minutes to gain entry, and hopefully just a few more to completely exit. What did you have in mind, Robby?"

"Let's send the room service agent up to Shifty's suite. As soon as he enters the room, Mac will lock the door from the outside. That will prompt maintenance and the security guard to go and take a look. Chops can keep the front desk agent busy with some mindless banter…"

"Three a.m.," says Chops.

"What?" asks Robby.

"Three a.m. That's when the bellman takes his break. He heads down the street to grab some grub and comes back. He gives himself about 30 minutes. You said 'recon,' right?"

"Yup. Fine work there, Chops," says Robby. "I'll go with you, Jake. I'll be your lookout and let you know when it's safe to return."

Jake nods. "Three a.m. it is," he says to Mac. "Last thing: Whatever camera covers the area around where I'll be heading down will need to be blacked out."

"Sure thing," says Mac.

"And Mac?" says Jake.

"Yeah, boss?"

"Can I talk to you for a second?"

"Yeah, sure."

"We'll be right back," says Jake to the other two as he leads Mac out of the suite and into the corridor. Robby gives Chops a look, Chops shrugs his shoulders.

"Is everything all right?" Jake asks. "You were quiet in there. If you're not up to this, just tell me, I'll understand. We'll understand."

"I'm good," insists Mac. "I think it's just the heat getting to me."

"I think it's getting to us all. OK, I just wanted to make sure," Jake said, "because I want you to know how much you mean to me, and how appreciated you are. Your contributions to the crew cannot be overstated, and don't ever forget that."

"I won't, boss," says Mac, as an apprehensive expression comes over him.

"Good. Let's get back in and rest before we head down."

CHAPTER 18

GOING UNDERGROUND

It's 2:30 a.m. when Jake, the only one who decides not to rest his weary head, wakes up the men. "Let's go, gentlemen, let's get ready now."

So the men scramble to get dressed and collect all the gear they will need, which isn't much beyond a couple of flashlights, earbuds for communicating, and a duffle bag to carry the dagger in. Mac will remain in the suite while he manipulates the hotel's internal system to send a meal to Shifty, which he does promptly at 2:35 a.m. Shifty will be getting a ribeye steak, an order of steak fries, some asparagus, apple pie, and a bottle of Dom Perignon, all compliments of the house. The scheduled delivery time is 3:00 a.m.

Therefore, at 2:45 a.m., Jake heads for the Tower and Chops makes his way to the front desk, while Robby plants himself 15 meters from Shifty's door to report on scene.

At 2:58 a.m., a kid, mid-twenties, scrawny, pushes the food cart just outside of Shifty's suite, then nervously gives the door three hard knocks. No answer. He gives it three more. Through the door, a muffled voice calls out, "What the…"

A moment later Shifty swings the door open, visibly agitated, looking down at the kid and says, "What's this shit? It's three o'clock in the mothafuckin' morning!"

"I'm so sorry," said Brad (so his nametag states), I have an order here," he says, looking at a receipt, "for a Shifty Lame, compliments of the house."

"It's Lane! Shifty Lane! Not Lame, you dumbass!"

"My deepest apologies, sir," said the young man.

"Get yo ass in here."

Brad pushes the cart into the suite, and the door closes. Robby immediately signals the group, so Mac can lock the door. He does.

Five minutes pass when maintenance and the lone security guard show up at the door.

Robby high-steps it to the Tower; the operation is underway.

The city's pulse is rapid, but luckily for them the hotel's is not. Robby arrives and posts up behind Jake. The coast is clear, and in a flash, Jake lifts the hatch and begins climbing down into the unknown abyss beneath the surface.

The tunnel is dark and mysterious, and built caringly sufficient, but with crude devices, and done effectively enough to create a workable path; a path that perhaps leads to a priceless treasure. There's an inch or so of water at their feet, which makes sense given the hotel's close proximity to the ocean.

Jake moves cautiously as his vision is slightly obstructed, even with the benefit of the flashlight steadfastly bright and facing forward. After nearly a hundred years, it's the dust, fog, water, and mist that make up most of the moving elements in the tunnel. And, of course, CO_2.

Chops is now chatting up Jena A., a breathtaking brunette beauty with an intoxicating sweet voice and bright, icy blue eyes. So it won't be a problem for Chops to spend as much time as he needs talking to her. If anything, he's giving her an escape from the tedium of working so late, or early, depending on how one would frame it. As he asks her for useless information pertaining to the city and hotel, the bellman strolls up to interject.

"Can I get you anything, Jena? I'm going to grab something small down the street, maybe bring back a coffee."

"No thanks, Harold," she replies.

"OooK," he said, and turns and walks away and out the front entrance.

Chops takes a step back and reports that the bellman is gone.

"I'm sorry," says Jena, "do you talk to yourself often?"

"Oh, no, sorry," he said, "I'm training to be an actor...was just practicing while you were busy talking to that gentleman."

"Well, Mr..."

"Wayne. Bruce Wayne," says Chops.

"Seriously? Are you still practicing?" Jena asks. "Are you playing Batman?"

"Maybe someday," he says, "So where are you from?"

"Boston," said Jena.

"What a coincidence, so am I!"

"Would you look at that," she said with a wide smile.

Jake is now an estimated 30 meters from where the prize is believed to be hidden. The air quality has noticeably diminished, and he lets out a violent cough, and then another one, so he stops momentarily to reset himself. He takes a pair of breaths, pauses, and moves on.

As he does, he notices that the water has risen to above his ankles. He slushes forward with 20 meters to go.

Within a few more steps, Jake's flashlight pointing straight ahead illuminates the end-wall, finally. And while he does, he brings to light an image causing his heart to stop. What he sees is a marble stone standing perpendicular, about four meters high and about a foot in diameter with a smooth, level surface on top. Resting on that plane is a small, rectangular chest with a thick, gold emblem fixed at its center. The symbol is the Spanish coat of arms, and depicts a lion on the right and an eagle on the left, each facing inward and surrounding the crown worn by her majesty Queen Isabella I of Castile. One could attest that the chest by itself, given its age, physical properties, and symbolism, is worth a fortune.

On its front is a key fittingly lodged in its hole. Inside this obscurely placed box is believed to be what Jake and the team are looking for.

With the conditions becoming increasingly more unbearable, Jake wastes no time in turning the key. He opens the box and there it is, wrapped in a cloth for added protection, as shiny as the Queen originally had it fashioned: the dagger of Christopher Columbus.

After a minute or so of admiring the treasure, Jake calls up to the crew, "I have it. I'm coming up."

He begins to walk back, and this time, with an extra hop in his step. When he reaches the ladder, he still has not heard from Robby.

Jake lets out a cough.

"Robby, do you copy? I'm ready to come up, is it clear?" asks Jake.

A few minutes elapse, and not a word. Jake begins to lose his balance and grips the ladder tightly.

"OK, listen," says Jake, "I'm going up. I have no choice."

Jake climbs and reaches the top, places his hand on the latch door and pushes, but can't get it to move. He's gasping for air while he closes his eyes. His grip on the ladder loosens, and his left hand begins to slide downward. His head tilts backward, and then suddenly it swings open. It's Robby at the top. He says, "I had a small crowd here, sorry." As he helps Robby grab a hold of his forearm, Jake does the same, and he hoists him back up. He walks around to the first step and sits. After a few minutes, Jake's breathing becomes easier. When Robby joins him after closing up the hatch and covering it with the plywood and carpet, Jake says, "Let's get out of here, mate."

CHAPTER 19

WE HAVE IT

It's the Grand Beach Hotel in Miami. It's there that Jake reserved a room the following day to use as a home base until business is completed.

Jake keeps to the plan and calls the number Carlos has been calling him from all the while, the other three look on. After a couple of rings, someone answers, and this time it's Carlos. "Go ahead," he says.

"I have what you're looking for," says Jake.

"I knew you would," says Carlos. "I just knew you would. Let us meet, shall we?"

"I want to hear her voice first."

"My pleasure, Mr. Jake."

A moment later, Amelia is on the line. "Jake," she says more calmly than the last time they spoke. "I'm OK," she says.

"Did they hurt you, baby?"

"No, I'm OK," she says. "I just want to go home."

"I know, baby, soon, I promise, this will all be behind us."

"OK."

Carlos cuts in. "Was that to your liking?"

"Yes," says Jake in an icy tone.

"Good," Carlos says. "Now, there is a place on the Strip called News Café. My associate will meet you there tomorrow at 2:00 p.m."

"No," says Jake.

"I'm sorry?"

"That's not going to work for us," answers Jake. "So here's how it's going to go down: I'll be at the Grand Beach Hotel over on Collins. You bring Amelia to me. Once I get her back in one piece, we'll meet and make the exchange, the dagger for the cash. But I need to see her first."

Carlos sighs and utters, "You really are in no position to negotiate, Jake. Are you sure you want to proceed this way?"

"That's gonna be the way of it, or you'll find your precious blade at the bottom of the Atlantic, followed by you and your crew."

The threat draws a chuckle from Carlos, who then says, "I can't figure out if I like you or despise you, Jake. But OK, I can accommodate this, since you've been so cooperative. But I'm warning you, Jake, do not try any funny business."

"Bring her, 2:00 p.m. tomorrow to room 318," says Jake, and then hangs up.

CHAPTER 20

SOMETHING UNEXPECTED

Just moments after hanging up with Carlos, Jake addresses Mac. "Tomorrow at noon, you're going to take the dagger away from this place, in your van, and stay with it until I say it's OK to move. There's a warehouse on NW Avenue that makes deliveries using the same type van as yours, so you'll blend in nicely."

"OK," answers Mac.

The following morning, Jake pulls Chops aside discreetly and says to him, "I want you to rent a vehicle and tail Mac today."

Chops is noticeably taken aback and asks, "Mac? Why?"

"I trust him, but he's not himself lately, and I need this to go down as smoothly as possible. Plus, if he's made, I want someone to tell me," Jake says. "Will you do this for me?"

"Of course, boss. Of course."

"Good," said Jake, placing his hand on Chops' shoulder.

At 11:45 a.m. Jake hands the duffle back to Mac and says, "Keep it safe."

"I will," Mac says, before he leaves the hotel room.

Chops is already waiting for Mac in the hotel garage. To be as clandestine as possible, he's rented a silver Toyota Camry, which is among the most popular cars driven in South Florida. He's parked and ready when Mac enters his driver's side door with the duffle bag in his right hand. He disappears to the back, then returns and starts the engine. Off he goes, backing out and heading toward the exit. A black Ford pickup moves behind him; that's Chops' cue to start moving.

Chops does his best to stay within two cars, and he's greatly successful as he's a near pro at tailing people, given his extensive experience in blackmailing his subjects.

After a 10-minute drive, Mac makes it to the warehouse and idles between two similar looking white vans. Chops is a good 50 meters away, behind him and across the street. He delivers his message via text to Jake to avoid using the radio that all four men are on. He texts "Set."

An hour evaporates with nothing to report by anyone, when Mac decides to move to the rear of the van and, without any windows to look through, it's impossible to know what he's doing. Chops is perplexed, but there's no reason for alarm, so he sits and waits. Twenty minutes or so later, Mac returns to the front, starts the truck and backs out. Now there's cause for concern. Chops texts Jake, "He's on the move."

Jake answers, "Follow."

Chops does so carefully. Mac takes a route bringing them back to the beach and toward the marina. He finds a spot, parks, and exits, leaving the duffle bag in the van. Chops never enters the marina. Instead, he parks a good distance away and uses his binoculars to witness Mac's movements. He sees Mac approach the San Luis; it's a grandiose, 150' luxury yacht complete with five bedrooms, a master suite, lounge area and, not astonishingly, a room reserved for nautical antiquities only, including artifacts such as vintage harpoons and spears, compasses, wheels and attire, to name a few.

There's also a chopper sitting on a pad at the stern of the great ship.

From Chops' point of view, Mac stands outside calling up to it until a door hatch opens to reveal Hector and another gentleman who's much larger, and more grave-looking for certain. It's one of Carlos' bodyguards. They walk down the gangway to meet him. After a brief discussion, Carlos and Mac shake hands. Carlos says, "Follow me."

The guard gestures to Mac and says, "After you."

The three men walk up and onto the yacht. As they enter, the guard closes the door, then tells Mac to spread his arms and legs out. The guard pats him down. Upon completion, the guard states, "He's clean."

It's now 1:35 p.m., and time is getting tight. Chops alerts Jake via text once again, and this time Jake uses the radio and calls to Mac and says, "Mac, do you copy?" But there's no response. "Do you copy, Mac?"

After a few seconds of silence, Jake says over the radio, "The bastard turned his radio off."

Chops sighs, leans back, and shakes his head in disgust. "What do we do now?" asks Chops.

"I'm workin' on it," said Jake.

CHAPTER 20

LET'S MAKE A DEAL

Mac is now in the company of Carlos, and the two sit directly across from one another. Also present is the guard who escorted Mac in, and Hector who is setting up refreshments. Carlos has a very relaxed and unperturbed aura about him, as he should, by playing the role as a gangster, and a boss…a powerful one, at least in his mind. Hector, conversely, is visibly tense and sits on the edge of his seat.

Carlos says to Mac, "My associate tells me you wish to make a deal?"

"That's right," says Mac.

"Do tell what you're offering."

"The dagger, and in exchange, I want $7.5 million."

"And do you have the dagger?" asks Carlos.

"Yes."

"Where is it?"

Mac says, "It's not with me."

"I can see that," says Carlos as he stands up and places his hands in his pocket. "I'm standing in front of a man who claims he has the dagger and who is prepared to betray his friends for money…you can see why I'm a little suspicious, no?"

Mac becomes increasingly fidgety and says, "Look, I'll go down to $7 million. Do we have a deal?"

Carlo says, "Mac, Mac, my new friend. Here's what I think. You're either here to set me up—"

"No, I'm not," Mac interrupts.

"Let me finish. You're either here to set me up, or you really are trying to undercut your friends who've been, I'm guessing, very good to you up to this point." He goes on, "So I'll tell you what, tell me where the dagger is, and then we can talk about a deal. I'm not going to ask you again."

"I can't do that."

Carlos faces the guard and with a flick of his finger signals him to leave.

"Where's he going?" Mac asks nervously. But Carlos ignores him, and after a few seconds elapse, the guard returns with another, dressed in the same suit and just as wicked -looking. They each grab an arm of Mac's and prop him up against his will. Carlos instructs them, "Take him downstairs and beat him until he's ready to talk." With that, they drag him through a swinging door and disappear.

Back at the hotel room, Jake and Robby wait for Amelia, but since Mac has gone off and seemingly betrayed them, the men are ready for anything. It's nearly 2:00 p.m., and Jake grabs a handgun from a backpack and cocks it, then tucks it into his waistband on his backside. He grabs another, does the same and hands it to Robby.

Robby is noticeably apprehensive and says, "You think I'll need this?"

"I hope not, mate," Jake says, "but we have to plan for the worst here."

"I understand."

Below deck in the only unkempt quarters on the yacht sits Mac, tied to a chair with his hands knotted behind his back. He's bloodied and bruised as he receives blow after blow to the head and midsection during his interrogation by the two guards. There's no way out now for Mac. Whether he tells of the whereabouts of the dagger or not, in his mind he's not getting off that boat alive.

Carlos decides to join the party. He stands over Mac and asks him calmly, "Where is the dagger?"

"Do we have a deal?" Mac asks, and follows the question with a kind of laughter from a man who's given up. But he hasn't fully thrown in the towel, not yet, as the tech genius has one more trick up his sleeve. Behind his back, he grates his Apple Watch with his opposite wrist. It's significant, because his watch will reactivate his radio to alert his team to what's transpiring. It's a final act of redemption, although likely too late. It was a monumental mistake for Carlos to not take his watch off, but few would think to do that.

"You were never going to pay us," says Mac, attempting to lure Carlos into a conversation and admit his nefarious intentions. Just then, Mac hits the sweet spot on his watch. His radio is hot, and Carlos can't help but take the bait. He's arrogant and a conversationalist, but also a consummate boaster, a trait harbored by most who seek to prove how strong and tough they really are. So Carlos can't resist.

Jake is alert and hears Mac's radio go on. He brings his finger to his lips to quiet Robby.

Now they listen intently.

"I suppose it matters not what I tell you now," Carlos says, "It's true, I used you and your crew to steal the dagger. The plan was to eliminate all loose ends, and it looks like it will begin with you. You mustn't take it personally, Mac. Don't you understand? The value of this treasure is too great to risk by keeping you alive. You and your crew would have known too much. It had to be this way. So in just a few moments, my men will storm the hotel, kill Jake and your friends, and eventually you, once you tell me where the dagger is!"

"And the girl? What did you do to her?"

Behind Carlos, a door opens. Carlos moves aside to reveal Amelia. She's unharmed; in fact, she looks well taken care of, but her impatient demeanor says something else. "Why don't you ask her yourself?" said Carlos.

Amelia takes a few steps closer to Mac and says, "Now, listen to me very carefully," she began. "You're not going to be afforded the same charities that Carlos has been giving you. So tell me where the dagger is, or I'll cut off a finger."

Mac, who's visibly shocked, says, "He cared for you. Who the hell are you?"

"My name is Amelia Esteban," she says, "wife to Carlos Esteban, niece to Nicola D'Agostino, who I also work for. This operation began long ago, and it is mine. I orchestrated it from the day I met Jake at the museum to now. You see, I want the dagger, and I want my uncle to sell it for me. He gets a piece, we get a piece, so we all win…except you, of course, and your friends. But Jake said he was quitting. He said he'd pulled off his last job. He doesn't decide when to quit, we decide. And his last job is the dagger. So if you think you're going to turn it upside down on me now, you're sorely and painfully mistaken. Watch, I'll show you."

Amelia looks at a guard and nods. The guard goes behind Mac and snaps off his right thumb with a wire cutter. Mac writhes and cries out in pain.

"Nine more to go, Mac," says Amelia. "You have five seconds."

Mac hangs in there, stays mum. "Take another one," Amelia commands. The guard again moves behind Mac and snaps off his right forefinger. Mac is thrashing and wailing, then screams, "OK, I'll tell you! I'll tell you!" Mac collects himself as best he can, then says, "It's in the van, the white one, just outside. License plate G347YT. Keys are in my pocket."

A guard rifles through his pockets and retrieves the set of keys. Carlos says to the guard, "Go now." The guard leaves. And to Mac he says, "A wise choice, my friend."

"I'm sorry," says Mac.

"Don't be sorry, Mac," says Carlos, "These things always have a way of working out."

"I'm sorry, Jake, I'm so sorry," Mac says.

"Jake?" asks Amelia.

Confused, Amelia examines Mac and pats him down once again and finds nothing, until she feels his watch.

"It's his watch!" shouted Amelia. She asks a guard for a gun and points it at Mac's forehead.

Mac calls out, "Jake! Get out of there, they're coming for you!"

Amelia pulls the trigger. Pop! She puts one through his forehead.

Jake, listening in, is stunned and saddened by the revelation, and his change of emotions are enough to divert his attention away from whoever is on the way. So in that split second when the door busts open, Jake and Robby are caught off guard. It's two men, each wasting no time in firing off rounds. While Jake blindly returns fire, he manages to drop one of them, and then is able to take cover behind a sofa. Robby, who was closest to the door, is a sitting duck. He's hit three times in the chest and once in the head. He collapses immediately to the floor...Robby is dead.

Now there's a standoff. The remaining hitman is perched just behind a wall between the closet and the door. He calls out in a thick Spanish accent and says, "They told me you would be difficult to shoot, so I brought this." He holds up a small round device, similar to a grenade. He tosses it and says, "Catch!" as he quickly exits the room. The device falls just to the right of Jake. Nearly simultaneously, he gets up and runs full speed toward the balcony when it explodes, engulfing the suite in flames and projecting Jake off the balcony, down three stories before he splashes awkwardly into the pool.

On the yacht, Carlos voices his displeasure with Amelia, saying, "What if he was lying about the dagger? What if it's somewhere else?"

"He was too weak to lie."

Just then, the door opens. It's the guard who went to retrieve the dagger. "We have it," he says with a big grin.

"See," says Amelia, "I told you so."

Carlos' cell phone rings. He answers, smiles, then hangs up and says, "Jake is dead."

Amelia feels the pull of two emotions: Elation and sadness, and the combination is visible on her face. Carlos, who's none the wiser, says, "Let's go celebrate."

"Wait," she says, "One still remains."

"We cut the head of the snake off, no one remains," he says. "Now, let's go celebrate."

"OK."

CHAPTER 21

A BEAST HAS AWOKEN

Down by the Port of Miami, Chops is still in his car waiting for instructions from Jake. Then he's surprised when Jake creeps up on his car on the passenger side, opens the door, and sits down quickly. But Jake immediately signals to Chops to be quiet, and then brings his finger to his ear to let him know they could still be listening. So Chops takes his earpiece out and turns his radio off.

"They think I'm dead, I want to keep it that way," said Jake.

"And Robby?"

"He didn't make it," Jake says. "It's just you and me."

A somber expression washes over Chops' face. He lowers his head and says, "I can't believe it. I just can't. What on earth do we do now?"

"I'm thinking."

"I'm sorry about your girlfriend...how it all turned out," says Chops.

"Nah, mate," Jake says, "I always knew there was something off about that bitch. She got me good, though. She definitely got me good." And after a brief passing of silence, Jake says, "You know what, Chops?"

"What's up?"

"I never had the opportunity to avenge my parents' deaths. These people, Carlos and his associates, they're going to wish they never met me."

That last statement makes the hairs on the back of Chops' neck stand on end, and sends a chill down his spine. Jake now appears as a man with nothing to lose and one who is ready to channel all of his hatred and direct it toward Carlos and anyone associated with him. Chops' friend is an entirely different animal now as he sits next to him. He's an uncaged beast, with a ravenous appetite for only one thing: vengeance.

Jake says, "Let's move. I got an idea."

"Where we headed?"

"Davie."

"What's in Davie?"

"We're going shopping."

The two enter the South Florida Arms and Range. They peruse the store and pile up a cart with handguns, clothes for cover, and radios among other items. Once finished, they head back to Miami to the marina and rent a small, 13-foot rowboat.

Next, they book a room at the Miami Marina Suites where Jake finally rests his head, and does so for several hours until Chops wakes him at 2:30 a.m. At such time they begin to get ready and dressed and head to Chops' car with all the gear. They load it back up and drive to the marina where the rowboat sits. Chops passes the equipment to Jake as he lays it down in the boat, one piece at a time.

It's 3:30 a.m.

Jake says, "See you in a bit," to Chops.

"Remember," says Chops, "When we left, there were three guards, Carlos, Hector, and Amelia left on board. I have no idea about a captain."

"I'll know soon enough."

Chops asks, "Are you sure you're all right?"

Jake nods, and says, "Your hands are clean…mine were never meant to be, and I'm at peace with that. Now, I'm going to bring them hell, every last one of them. Meet me back here in a couple of hours."

"I will, and good luck."

Jake nods again, then boards the boat and immediately begins rowing out to sea.

At this time, the San Luis has made its way off shore, roughly three kilometers northeast of South Beach and remains anchored in the still waters of the Atlantic. Jake rows to within fifty meters when he takes a necklace out of his front pocket. Aside from a handgun and the clothes on his back, it's all that was salvaged from the explosion in the hotel. He opens it to reveal the picture one last time. By his expression, it's obvious that the photo was of days past, and now he has a more focused and determined look as he fixates on the locket.

After a few minutes, Jake places the locket back in his pocket and begins to change into his black attire, then fastens a pair of holsters to his belt and inserts two Berettas with silencers attached to them and four extra clips, along with two blades, one four-inch and one six-inch. Lastly, he draws black mud and runs his fingers down from his forehead to his neckline. He's ready for war.

Jake rows the boat right to the starboard side, away from the windows, and ties the boat to a dinghy hanging from the yacht. He takes another rope, this one coiled around his shoulder with a hook attached, and flings it up onto the yacht and pulls it back until it catches the railing. He gives it a couple of good tugs to ensure its strength, and then begins to climb up.

CHAPTER 22

BRINGING THE HELL

At the top of the rope now, Jake climbs over the railing. Right foot down, then the left drops gently, and he's undetected. So he creeps quietly hugging the edge of the yacht, ducking every window he passes and pausing to listen to sounds. It doesn't take long for him to spot a guard who's leaned back in a chair with his feet on the railing, facing the ocean.

Within a few meters of the guard, Jake takes cover in a corner, the last spot before the stern becomes the port side of the boat. There's a small pot of sand with beach rocks resting on top. A cheesy decoration, but useful for Jake. He takes a rock and tosses it gently, and when it hits and rolls across the deck, it does so with enough noise to alert Guard #1 from his rested position. He sits up and calls out, "Who's there?"

There's no answer, so he steps slowly into the direction of his worst nightmare. "Hello?" he calls out again. And again hears nothing. He continues on until he reaches the rock. He's past where Jake is huddled, and he picks up the rock and oddly examines it, but he will wish he hadn't. Jake swiftly runs up behind him and cups his left hand around the guard's mouth and, before the guard can react, Jake runs a blade across his throat. The guard slowly drifts off to death while a stream of his blood runs down his front. Jake lets him down calmly to the deck. He grabs his radio and presses the "call button" and quickly lets it go. It's enough to send a signal to the other guards. The dead guard receives a transmission, "Go ahead." And then again, "Go ahead." With no response, he begins to make his way to the area previously occupied by Jake's first victim. As he comes around the bow, he clearly sees his partner on the ground and lying in a pool of his own blood. So he rushes toward the guard and kneels next to him and checks his pulse. He's gone. Guard #2 stands, looks around frantically, and draws his gun. When he turns around and looks in the direction he came from, a blade comes hurled in his direction and sticks in his chest, precisely where his heart lies. He drops fast, but his impulse causes him to discharge his gun. Jake retrieves his blade and wipes it on his victim.

Now there are two guards down, but the discharge has awakened the rest of the boat's occupants.

Guard #3 has been asleep in his own cabin. He opens his eyes hard, jumps out of bed, throws on a pair of pants, grabs a gun, and begins carefully patrolling.

This guard is big, bulky, and now aware that something is not right. He knows where the shot came from, and that it could spell trouble, so his peripheral senses are heightened as he walks up a staircase and onto the top deck. He also knows the yacht and what looks out of place, and right now, the shadow protruding from the port side is just that. He edges along slowly until he's within a few meters. He makes his move and rushes around a corner, then stops suddenly to see a guard standing up, propped up by Jake, who tosses the body toward the third guard, distracting him enough to charge him.

In a flash, Jake grabs ahold of the guard's gun hand and delivers two powerful elbows to his face and rips the gun away. But the guard won't go down easily, and they square off. The two punch, block, and kick each other repeatedly, and begin grappling on the deck. Jake reaches for his gun, but the guard impedes him by grabbing his wrist. Then Jake turns him over, causing the guard to release the weapon. All in one motion, Jake points the gun at the guard and fires three silent rounds into his chest. He falls to his knees, then forward, and face down. He's dead.

Jake is out of breath. The noise of the tussle has provoked Hector to stumble upon the scene. He's frozen in fear. While Hector is motionless, Jake stands and walks gingerly toward him. Hector puts his arms up and stutters, "I knew nothing, I swear."

"Sure you did."

"Jake, please…"

But his plea falls on deaf ears, as Jake wastes no time in raising his weapon and pulling the trigger once, putting a bullet just above Hector's unibrow and through his head. He drops like a sack of potatoes. But behind him is Carlos, and he has a gun and fires it at Jake. The bullet grazes Jake's arm, causing him to twirl around, but he's able to retreat to the bow.

During this time, Amelia has barricaded herself inside her suite with explicit instructions from Carlos to not leave until he says it's safe.

Carlos now walks and has the distinct advantage of following a trail of dripping blood from Jake's upper left arm. He slowly creeps and shadows the red stains. Around the bow he goes, to the port side. The trail continues to a doorway. But just outside that doorway lies Jake's first pair of victims. And with even more blood spilled around the bodies, Jake has cleverly hidden his tracks by mixing his trail of blood with theirs. A despondent Carlos turns the handle and nudges the door, but it's locked, so he releases it and hangs back. Then he cranes his neck to get a closer look through a small circular window in the door. There's a staircase leading down, but that's it. It's eerily quiet. Just when Carlos is about to straighten his back to resume his hunt, the point of a spear crashes through the small, round window and continues through Carlos' left eye and out the back of his head. Jake had stumbled upon the "antiquities room," and took full advantage of it. He walks up the stairs, unlocks the door and uses some oomph to push it open, as Carlos' corpse remains propped up and dangling with the spear half in the door and all the way through his noggin.

Jake leaves him hanging, latterly, and climbs over the side of the boat, and heads back to shore.

Jake returns to shore in the rowboat. There to meet him is Chops, who says, "How'd it go?"

"Went great."

"So…" says Chops, "Everyone gone?"

"Not yet."

At the same time Jake arrives on shore, Amelia has left the safety of her cabin and carefully walks around the carnage left behind by Jake. She comes upon Carlos and places her hands to her mouth momentarily before her attention is drawn by the sight of a necklace hanging down from the pointy end of the blood-soaked spear at the back of Carlos' head. She knows it; it's the locket she gave to Jake on their way down to Miami. The visual brings terror to every fiber of her being.

When she's finally gone through the corpse-filled vessel and feels no eminent threat from Jake, she sits on a small staircase that leads to the landing pad for the chopper. She holds the locket, opens it, and looks on with sadness before she cracks a subtle grin. It's emotional for her. But then, something happens that brings the terror back to Amelia. The locket begins to countdown, three, two, one...the San Luis blows up in a colossal mountainous ball of fire, and Amelia with it. Large pieces of the vessel are sent flying, while the remainder of the ship is engulfed in flames. It's a showcase for all of Miami's early risers to see, thanks to the charger Jake stuck to the side of the yacht on his way up the rope on his initial climb.

"Yup," says Jake, "They're all gone."

CHAPTER 23

ABOUT THAT DAGGER

Already the air seems clearer, and Jake and Chops can breathe knowing that the worst is behind them. However, as they sit across from one another at a waterfront café, each with a coffee placed in front of them, Chops says, "It's too bad after all that, the dagger is lost forever. It's a shame, really."

"Who says it's lost forever?"

"Wasn't it on the boat when it exploded?"

"A dagger was on that boat, but not *the* dagger," says Jake.

Chops looks confused, and Jake begins to grin. "Well, this I have to hear," says Chops.

"Before you arrived in Miami," says Jake, "I went and paid a visit to the Florida Blade Creators in Miramar. I brought the picture of the dagger to the dealer and asked for a replica to be made. Carlos and his lackeys never had a clue what it looked like, they could only go by what that diary had, and maybe if they were smart, they had what I had: an actual picture. And even if they did, it was inconceivable that he knew the finer details of the blade. He wasn't as smart as he let on, and I could see that the moment I sat down with him."

"Jesus," says Chops.

Jake goes on, "I asked only of one favor from the knife dealer, and after I gave them a few extra bucks, he agreed that there was to be no trademarks or company logos or insignias on the thing. And so it was made just the way I wanted it. It was a mere image of the one I had in the encyclopedia. And he had it done in two days."

"Wait a minute," says Chops. "So, what did you bring back up from the tunnel?"

"Nothing. I went down just so I knew this thing was real, and then I left it there."

Chops leans back and nods to indicate it's all adding up now. "That's why you let Mac take the dagger away from here," says Chops. "It wasn't so priceless after all."

"That's right."

"And the chest?"

"Also a replica of the original, made by the dealer," Jake says. "In fact, when I went down in the tunnel, the fake chest and dagger were already in my bag, but no one knew. I thought it best to keep it to myself until the time was right."

"You sly bastard," says Chops jokingly. "So, when do we go back and get the real dagger?"

"Depends."

"On what?"

"What are you doing tonight?"

Chops smiles from ear to ear and says, "Not a thing."

Twenty-four hours later, Jake and Chops visit the hotel and, since they know all they need to, there's no reason to reserve a suite. In a matter of minutes, with Chops looking out, Jake goes back down in the tunnel, retrieves the dagger and comes back up.

"What do we do with it?" asked Chops.

"I already made a call to my Pops. We have a buyer, and his name is Honk."

"So what's next, then?"

"What's next?" says Jake. I have a little business I need to attend to in Boston."

CHAPTER 24

HIS FINAL ACT

It's a beautiful, sunny day, and the streets of Boston's North End are packed, teeming with tourists and locals alike enjoying the eateries and gift shops, or just perusing around and taking in its authentic charm. A tall, well-dressed gentleman walks exasperatedly with his head down through the thick crowd. He comes up upon Francesco's Pizzeria, an Italian restaurant famous for its "old country" cuisine and highlighted by its gourmet pizza.

Inside, the place feels vastly different than the boisterous activity happening outside on the streets and sidewalks. It's eerily quiet, as there are no customers welcome on this day of celebration. Directly to the left a bartender leans on his elbow and watches a sporting event on TV, although the volume is nearly all the way down. He's the only one visibly present, so the man asks him, "Is he here?"

The bartender, Johnny, props himself up from his slumber and says, "He's in back, Rocco."

Rocco takes a deep breath and apprehensively makes a beeline for the back room. When he gets there, he stands directly in front of Nick.

"What news do you have for me?" asks Nick.

"I'm afraid it's not good. We had complications," says Rocco uneasily.

"What kind of complications?"

"May I sit?"

"No," says Nick, "no, you may not."

Rocco takes a deep breath. "I'm sorry, Nick, but no one made it. There was an explosion, you see…"

"An explosion?"

On the yacht." He says more tensely now, "Your niece was on it."

"My niece was on that idiot Carlos' boat, and it blew up?" asked Nick. "Is that what you're telling me?"

"Yes."

Nick says, "Are you saying my niece is…dead?"

Says Rocco, "I'm afraid so."

"And the dagger, was it also in the explosion?"

"It is believed that it was also on board, sir."

"So, what you're telling me is I have no niece and no dagger?" asks Nick.

"I'm sorry."

"You're sorry, huh? You're sorry. Well, that's just not going to help this matter. And what about Jake?"

Rocco says, "No one's really sure. It was believed he perished in the hotel, but…"

"But what?"

"His body was never found…and the night the yacht went up in flames, Carlos had made a distress call, and it sounded like he mentioned Jake's name."

"It sounded like it, huh? How does this sound?" said Nick, pointing at Rocco. "Leave, and do not return until you find out where he is, understand me? Because if this man is still above ground, it's going to be big trouble, not just for me, but for everyone. Understand me?"

"Yes, sir," said Rocco.

"Good."

Rocco turns and scampers out.

Nick says to himself softly, "Where are you, you bastard?"

Just then the lights flicker repeatedly, then go out. The cold steel of a gun barrel is pressed to Nick's right temple.

"I'm here," whispered Jake.

ABOUT THE AUTHOR

Marc Zappulla an American author from the Boston suburb of Medford, Massachusetts.

He was inspired to write his first novel *The Last Longshoreman* by his father's thirty-year career as a longshoreman on the Boston docks.

Zappulla currently lives in Boston and is busy working on his next book.

OTHER WORKS BY MARC ZAPPULLA

The Last Longshoreman
Unmasked by Gerry Cheevers
How a Champion is Made by Steve Cardillo
Active Girls, Heathy Women by Mai Tran

Made in the USA
Middletown, DE
26 April 2019